AWAY TO SEA

by the same author

THE BLACK BUCCANEER

DOWN THE BIG RIVER

LONGSHANKS

RED HORSE HILL

HE WAS PROMPTLY KNOCKED DOWN BY A BLOW
OF CREADON'S FIST

AWAY TO SEA

BY STEPHEN W. MEADER

ILLUSTRATED BY CLINTON BALMER

ISBN 978-1-931177- 60-3 cloth
ISBN 978-1-931177- 61-0 paperback

SOUTHERN SKIES

LITTLE ROCK, ARKANSAS

www.southernskies.com

Dedication

The republication of this book is dedicated to the memory of Vince Foster by his friend who misses him every day, Jerry Atchley.

TO MY WIFE

ILLUSTRATIONS

AWAY TO SEA

I

ORNING—and what a morning! Jim Slater paused in the middle of his breakfast and sat with the fork halfway to his mouth, looking out through the little square panes of the kitchen window. The sun's first beams were glinting on a million frosty twigs, and the two big elms in the yard looked like twin pillars in a cathedral of ice. But it was a spring sun— warm. Already the boy could hear a steady drip of melting snow from the eaves. Up in the woods across the river the sap must be running in the sugar maples. Time to tap some trees if he wanted to make syrup this year. If he

wanted to! That was the strange part of it. Somehow, this spring he had lost interest in the things that always delighted him before. What had got into him, anyway?

Thinking of maple syrup brought his attention back to the plate of golden-brown buckwheats in front of him. At least there was nothing wrong with his appetite. He helped himself to more pancakes and flooded them generously with syrup from the squat blue jug.

The door from the woodshed opened and Jonathan Slater's big frame filled it. He was a solid man, broad-shouldered, with a ruddy, bearded face. Reaching below his knees was his old miller's coat, white with the dust of many grindings.

"Looks like I'll be busy all day, Jim," said he, surveying his son. "Joel Steere's here already, with twenty bushel. I want you to fetch home that last load o' wood. Hitch up the bay team an' start soon's you can. Snow's goin' to melt off fast today, an' if we wait, the mud'll be hub-deep on that hill road."

"Ay, ay, sir," said Jim. The expression slipped out before he thought. It was not until he saw a slow frown deepening between his father's brows that he realized he had used it.

"I'm sorry, Father," he grinned, as he rose from the table. "Sure, I'll get the wood down here before noon."

"Very good," replied the older man seriously. "But let's have no more o' that seafarin' foolishness." And he turned and went back to his milling.

Jim stretched his arms and looked around the great, spotless kitchen. The stone fireplace, built by Grandfather Slater, filled one end of the room and the flames cast a comfortable glow along the broad pine boards of the floor. Above it, on two pegs over the mantel, rested the family's one visible heritage from Jim's other grandfather, Captain Jim Ballou of Salem. It was the battered brass spy-glass used by the old mariner until the day of his death. Ruddy, shining pots and pans of copper hung in a neat row beside the range, and shelves full of china and pewter gleamed cheerfully from a cabinet on the opposite side of the room. Why, Jim wondered, with a lump in his throat, should any one want to leave so beautiful a place? But he had been over all that many times before, and knew there was no answer.

Out in the stable the boy set himself to currying the big team of bays. He was whistling by the time the heavy work-harness had been flung on their backs. And he even sang a bar or two as he buckled the girths and hooked the trace-chains to the sturdy bob-sled that stood in the yard.

News must have gone up the valley that the Blackstone River had broken its bonds of ice and the water-wheel was turning at Slater's grist-mill. Already, when Jim swung his team out of the yard, there were three farmers' rigs hitched at the long rail. It would be a busy day and a profitable one.

The mill was the pride of his father's heart. Like the house, it was built solidly of stone and masonry. It had the biggest water-wheel in Rhode Island, and its fine burr-stones had been brought all the way from England. To it the farmers from miles around carried their wheat and corn to be ground. It had made Jonathan Slater one of the wealthy men of the community and it was a fixed idea with him that his only son should be the miller after him.

Out on the road Jim gave the bays their heads. As they hit a brisk, jingling trot the boy stood up and balanced himself on the swaying cross beam of the front sled. It was a favorite trick of his. He liked to think of himself as standing thus on the pitching deck of a vessel in rough weather. Most of Jim's imaginings had to do with the sea, for though he had never actually been aboard a ship in his life, he had heard his mother tell a thousand incidents of Old Jim Ballou's voyages. And he had read every book of sea adventure he could lay his hands on.

A mile down the valley road, Jim turned the horses up to the right, following a winding, snowy lane toward the top of the ridge. The wood lot to which he was going was high on the crest of Smoke Hill. From its top, a hundred years before, the Narragansett Indians had signaled with smoke to outposts of their tribe on the lower ground by the bay shore.

When the final pitch to the summit had been climbed, Jim blanketed the steaming bays and fell to work. He stacked the four-foot lengths of split oak trimly across the sled's string-pieces. A good cord and a half there was, but he got it all on, for this would be the last load of the winter. It was heavy work and he was glad to stretch his arms and rest for a moment when it was over.

The sun beckoned him to the southern brow of the hill. From there the land fell away, mile on mile of rolling woods and fields to the thin line of silver at the horizon, that he knew was Narragansett Bay. Close beside him on the ridge there was a giant sentinel pine. From its lofty top he might see still more. The broken stubs of branches invited him to climb and in a few moments he had swarmed his way upward another eighty feet.

The view, when he turned his head to look through a gap in the branches, had widened amazingly. He could see the tiny spires and smokes of Providence, now, and the bay was no longer a silver thread but a broad sheet of water, broken by points and islets. Close by the end of one of those rocky little islands he made out a speck scarce the size of a pin-head. At first he could not be sure that it was moving, but after two or three minutes its position had definitely changed, and instead of being gray it glinted white in the sun.

It was a sail—too far away to distinguish its shape or size, but a vessel of some kind. Jim wished he had brought his grandfather's telescope. Of course it might be only a coasting smack heading down to Newport or New Bedford. But then again it might be a bark, or a full-rigged ship, putting to sea in the fine March weather, bound for the Canaries or the Indies, or round the Horn to China.

The boy watched as long as the sail remained in sight.

When finally it disappeared around a headland he climbed slowly down and returned once more to the horses. The sun was swinging high in the south. If he was to reach home in time for dinner he would have to start at once.

His father had been right about the sledding. There was warmth in the sun that morning, and the snow was melting fast on the slopes. If the going had not been down-hill the big team might have had trouble with their heavy load. As it was, Jim walked the last quarter mile, guiding the toiling bays past the patches of bare dirt that now flecked the road.

He unhitched beside the wood-pile, led the team into the barn, and rubbed them down before he gave them their grain.

In the kitchen, Jim's father and mother were already at the table. Unlike Jonathan Slater, his wife was neither tall nor muscular. She was so slight that she looked almost frail, but she held herself very straight and there was a fearless directness in her blue eyes. Around her face, softening its outlines, were tendrils of graying hair.

She smiled at her big son. "Sit down, Jim," she said. "We didn't wait, because your father has so much to do at the mill. But Martha has a plate hot for you."

Jim washed his hands and joined his parents at the table. Before him Martha, the old servant, set smoking roast beef and potatoes. She moved to and fro, silent-footed in her moccasins. To Jim her wrinkled, brown, impassive face was as familiar as the chairs or the silver, for the old Gay Head Indian woman had been a member of the household since before he was born.

There was little conversation at the table that noon. Jim somehow did not feel like talking and the miller was too preoccupied with his own affairs to notice the boy's silence. As always, his mother was quiet, but her eyes studied Jim's face.

When the meal was over Jim went with his father to help with the grinding. It was his responsibility to keep a tally of the sacks of grain and pour them into the big hopper which fed the slowly moving stones. It was not hard work. As he slit the string at the top of each sack he would make a mark on a sheet of paper, opposite a farmer's name, then empty the grain into the maw of the hopper. When he came to the fifth bag he drew a diagonal line through the four marks and started a new series.

The burr-stones made a steady hum below him, and dust hung fragrantly in a bright haze where a beam of sun shone through the west window.

It was a pleasant, peaceful sort of task. If he followed his father's wishes he would settle down to it for the rest of his life. Jim scowled at the thought and shook himself. As yet he had no clear idea of the conflict that was going on inside him. All he felt was a queer, aching desire to be moving—a homesickness for far-off places.

Tomorrow, March 5, 1821, would be his seventeenth birthday. He was big enough to take care of himself—

and, he thought, to make his own decisions. He had finished school. Everything the little spectacled school-master in the village could teach him he had dutifully learned. Now, if ever, was the time to break away—before his father came to depend on him too heavily.

By sunset, the last of the day's grist was ground. Jim climbed down from his platform, wiping the dust from his cheeks and eyebrows. He wanted to get away somewhere by himself and battle this thing out. With a quart measure of waste grain, scooped up from the floor of the mill, he headed for the pigeon-loft in the barn. Here, alone with the preening, cooing birds, he could think.

Jim had no way of knowing that scores of other Yankee boys at that very moment were sharing the same problem—boys who a quarter of a century later would be officers of the fastest-sailing merchant ships the world has ever seen—the American clipper fleet. Up the coast and down, from Bangor to Baltimore, the call of the sea was strong that Spring.

All Jim knew was the misery of his own struggle. Obedience was part of his training, and if he carried out his half-formed plan, his father would suffer a stunning blow. On the other hand he had a feeling that his mother would understand him.

When at last it grew so dark that he could no longer see the pigeons, and their voices had subsided to an occasional crooning murmur, the boy went slowly down the ladder.

He was late for supper but nothing was said about it. Jonathan Slater was planning the morrow's work as he ate. "We'll get Ed Wilkins up from the village, first thing in the morning," he said, "and you two can go at that wood. We ought to have it all sawed and stacked up by the end of the week."

Jim kept his eyes on his plate. If he had had to answer his words would have choked him. In the sitting-room, when supper was over, he took a book and tried wretchedly to read by the light of the spermaceti candles. His father finished his newspaper and went early to bed, as usual. Jim managed a gruff "Good night." But when his mother laid aside her darning and rose, to follow him, the boy got suddenly to his feet and flung his arms around her in a long, fierce hug. She looked up at him tenderly and stroked his cheek, but she did not question him.

"Good night, my boy, and bless you," she murmured, and then Jim found himself alone.

For a long time he sat staring at his book, while the tall clock ticked away the minutes. Then he was conscious of a faint sound behind him and glanced up to see Martha standing in the doorway of the kitchen. Her face, as always, was a wrinkled mask, and her black, beady eyes gave no sign. But in both hands she bore a flat cake of Indian meal with a crisp brown crust. It was a bannock, one of Jim's favorite foods.

The old woman came close to his chair. "You goin'

away," she said impassively. "Ol' Martha make you breakfus'. Here—" and she held the bannock out to him.

As Jim took it from her she turned silently and padded out of the room. The boy stood looking after her a moment, open-mouthed in amazement. Then he grinned suddenly. "I guess that settles it," he muttered. "I'm going!"

In a drawer of his mother's old secretary he found paper and a quill pen. For the next half hour he labored over the most difficult letter he had ever had to write. When the dozen lines of the message were finished and signed with his name, he folded his note carefully and laid it on top of the darning-basket.

Then with the feelings of a criminal, he tiptoed off to bed.

Jim must have slept that night, but not for many hours. He lay for a long time thinking, restlessly. And when slumber finally overtook him he kept starting awake at intervals to look at his big silver watch.

The time he had fixed in his mind was four o'clock. At a quarter to four he woke suddenly and found the shrunken half of an old moon shining in the window. Shivering with excitement and the chill of the unheated room, he crawled out of bed and into his clothes. Heavy shoes he put on, and a warm jacket. His cap was downstairs and he was afraid of waking his father if he tried to get it. So, bareheaded, he crept out of the bedroom window and clambered down the huge ivy-trunk that had served him as a ladder on more than one escapade.

On the ground he stood for a minute, staring up at the venerable house, gray and quiet in the moonlight. Then he turned and set his face southward, toward the sea.

II

T HAD turned cold again in the night, and Jim's shoes crunched noisily in the snow. Moving with caution lest he should be heard, he left the yard and set out down the valley road. Soon he was able to quicken his stride. He hurried along by the light of the setting moon, and munched at Martha's bannock as he went.

Jim was tall and long-legged. The miles slipped behind him steadily. Except for the occasional challenge of some farmer's dog, roused by his passing step, he went without notice. A little after five he began to see lights glimmering as the householders rose to do their chores. And by five-thirty he was at the Forks of the Road, six good miles from home. There he waited, looking up the East Pike.

In a few moments he heard the crunching sound of wagon wheels that he had been expecting. It was Ben Derry, the carrier, jogging his old horse toward town. He brought the mail each day to the settlements up the valley. He was a friend of long standing and Jim knew he could be trusted. The carrier had been gunner's mate on a privateer in the War of 1812, and lost a leg in action. He stumped about on a brass-bound wooden peg, and could tell more stories of the sea, true or otherwise, than any man in the back country of Rhode Island.

He whistled when he saw Jim standing by the side of the road. "Well, well, my lad—ye're abroad early to-day!" he cried. "Shovin' off, eh? Weighin' anchor? Well, ye've a fine day for it. Come aboard then, and we'll make sail!"

Jim climbed to the wagon seat beside him. "No, I haven't much of a plan," he confessed, in response to a question from the carrier. "Yesterday I got a feeling I just had to go. I'm trusting to luck to find a ship in Providence, ready to sail. If not I'll have to keep on to Boston."

Ben Derry gave a chuckle. "I know just how it works," he said. "It's the Spring gittin' into yer blood. Same thing happened to me, only I was no more than a shaver half your size. It hit me all of a sudden like, an' off I went, an' never set foot in Ameriky ag'in for six year. D'yer folks know ye're goin'?"

"No," said Jim, hesitating. "At least—I suppose

they'll know soon. I left a note for Mother. That's why I've got to get a ship today. I'm running away."

The carrier nodded. He seemed to take this announcement as a matter of course. "We'll be in Central Falls by nine o'clock, an' ye can easy git to Market Square 'fore noon. Sorry I ain't goin' all the way to Providence."

The fat old horse plodded along at a pace that seemed painfully slow to Jim. Several times in the course of the next few miles he turned his head to watch the road behind them. But there was no sign of pursuit. Once they met a farmer from up Woonsocket way, who would surely have recognized the miller's son if he had not turned the collar of his jacket high about his face, and slouched back on his seat.

Ben Derry filled the three-hour ride with sage advice. He told Jim the duties of a 'prentice seaman and gave him so many pointers on forecastle etiquette that the boy's head fairly swam. Then he started in on ropes and rigs. This subject lasted till they were in the village of Central Falls, and he finished with a parting injunction not to ship aboard a "lime-juicer." He himself had been kidnaped by a British press-gang when he was a youth, and he had a special prejudice against cockney second officers.

"Well, matey," he said, as he clapped Jim on the shoulder, "a fine voyage to ye, an' may ye find a ship wi' soft hammocks an' plenty o' plum-duff on Sundays!"

When the creaking post-cart had driven off, Jim

started walking once more. He still had five or six miles to cover, for he took a little-used back road instead of the turnpike to town.

By the time he reached Providence he was hungry and glad of a chance to rest, so he entered a little shop at the foot of the hill on North Main Street and bought some crackers and cheese. Sitting on a horse-block by the curb, he made a very comfortable lunch. And as he ate he watched the farmers' wagons pass on the way to market, and the big dockside drays loaded with merchandise from far-off ports.

The hearty bustle of the first Spring weather was in the air. Tradesmen brushed off the brick pavement before their shops and set out their wares. Up in the churchyard behind him, Jim heard the chirp of an early robin. The boy could hardly wait to finish his meal and push on toward his adventure.

It was past twelve when he threaded his way among the stalls and wagons of the market and reached the wharves. From three blocks off he had seen the masts and spars of a big East Indiaman and it was toward her dock that he now hastened. A pair of longshoremen were taking their nooning in the sun on the pierhead.

Jim waited politely till a break in their conversation gave him his chance. Then he stepped forward. "Could you tell me," he asked, "if this ship is sailing today, and where I might find her captain?"

One of them stared at him dully and the other

laughed. "Lor', no!" he replied. "She ain't been in but two or three days, an' half her cargo's still aboard. Reckon she won't clear for another fortnight."

Jim was a little taken aback, but he thanked the dockers and inquired if they knew of any other vessels about to sail.

The stupid one merely shook his head in answer, but the livelier of the pair nudged his companion and looked at him with a sort of leering chuckle.

"Why, Bill," he said, "ye must be forgettin'. How about Cap'n Hack's schooner? Ain't she ready for sea?"

He turned back to Jim. "I take it, young man," said he, "that ye're fair anxious to git a berth, an' the quicker the better. Now ye take that schooner—the *White Angel*. No smarter skipper afloat than Jethro Hack, an' I shouldn't wonder if he might need a hand right now. Sailin' today, too, on the afternoon tide."

"A schooner?" asked Jim, a trifle doubtfully. "I wouldn't want to ship on a coasting boat—"

"Huh!" snorted the longshoreman. "The *White Angel*, she'll give ye all the deep-sea sailin' ye're after. She's bound fer Africa—the Ivory Coast—an' a cargo—" he nudged his friend again—"a cargo o' perfumes an' spices."

At this remark the two of them burst into a roar of laughter which might have given Jim pause if he had not been so excited.

"Africa! The Ivory Coast!"

"Where do you say this schooner lies?" he asked, impatient.

The docker grew sober at once. "Third pier down. Big, tall-masted craft, painted white. Ye'd best hurry!"

Jim needed no urging. He thanked the men and went down the wharfside at an eager trot. The shipping was crowded close, with a tangle of jib-booms and spars jutting out over the street, and Jim was fairly under the *White Angel's* figurehead before he recognized the schooner.

She was in ballast, riding high out of water. Her paint was badly weathered, and patches of gray barnacles along her waterline suggested a foul bottom. Yet Jim found something racy about her long, slim lines and the soaring height of her masts. There was an air of bustle among the men at work on deck that seemed to bear out the information Jim had about her early sailing.

A short gangplank ran from the dock to the waist of the vessel, and by the deck end of the plank a man lolled, smoking a cigar. He was a smallish fellow with a smooth-shaven face and shifting, ratty eyes that Jim instinctively disliked. However, there was a certain jauntiness about his glazed hat and pigtail. By his dress the boy judged him to be one of the ship's officers.

Jim went up the gangplank and stood before him. "Good morning, sir," he said. "Could I speak to the captain?"

The man looked him over coldly. "And wot," he asked, "might you be wantin' with the captain?"

"I'd like to ask him for a berth aboard this ship," Jim answered.

"Hm!" said the other, with a flash of interest. "Fore-mast hand?"

"Well, I've never been to sea before," the boy replied, "but I'm strong, and willing to learn. All I want is a chance."

The officer looked him up and down with a doubtful eye. "What we need," he said, "is seamen, not lubbers. This is no pleasure v'yage. We drive 'em, aboard the *White Angel*."

Jim did not like the cruel snap of the fellow's jaws as he finished this remark, but he could not see his chance slip away. "I'm not afraid of work," he said, and stood his ground.

The man gave him a queer look. "All right, my lad," he nodded, at length, "come along o' me."

Following the mate's swaggering figure, Jim went aft along the deck and down the four steps of the companion-way. Opposite the foot of the narrow stairs was a door, at which his conductor knocked lightly. At first there was no answer, and the man had to rap harder.

"Come in," growled a rasping voice, and the next moment the boy found himself in the cabin. It was a long, low chamber, lighted by a square port at either side of the rudder post, in the stern. Narrow doors in the bulkheads gave access, as Jim supposed, to the officers' sleeping quarters. There were chart racks and lockers along the sides between these doors, and a huge brass lamp hung from the deck beams above.

All these things the boy took in with his first fleeting glance. Then he saw the man sitting at the opposite end of the heavy table.

"Well?" snarled the hard voice again.

The mate was no longer jaunty. To Jim he seemed to shrink visibly in size. "Sorry to interrupt, sir," he said, in a half-whining voice. "This 'ere lad thinks 'e'd like to ship along of us, sir."

Captain Jethro Hack moved forward a trifle in his chair. He sat with his head held low between hunched shoulders, like some ruffled bird of prey. And his eyes, deep set under shaggy brows, made the similarity more striking. They glinted now with the same cold ferocity that Jim had once seen in the eyes of a captive eagle.

For several seconds the captain stared at the boy. "Greenhorn, eh?" he grated, finally. "Runaway, too, I'll warrant."

There was another pause and then suddenly he burst into a mirthless laugh. "Ho, ho, ho! We'll ship him, Mr. Jarvis. Ay, we'll show him the sea, an' a bit more besides. Sign him on, an' make a sailor of him. Don't put his dunnage for'ard, though. Let him sleep in the cuddy, an' in his spare time he can do the cabin work. I've missed it since old Cato died."

Evidently that ended the interview, for the captain slouched back in his chair again and his hand moved mechanically to the black rum bottle on the table before him.

"Ay, sir," Jarvis murmured, and pushed Jim before him out of the cabin. When he had closed the door he pointed along the short passageway at one side of the companion stairs. "Bring yer box aboard, an' stow it there in the cuddy," he said. "Then I'll 'ave ye sign the articles."

"There isn't any box," Jim answered. "All I own is what I've got on."

The mate looked at his clothes, frowning. "Well, I suppose we've got to find ye an outfit, then," he said. "Stay right 'ere, now, an' don't ye go off a-talkin' to the crew."

In three or four minutes he was back with a blanket, an old pair of sea-boots, and a sou'wester hat. Along with these he brought a folded, greasy-looking document and a pen. The papers bore a long list of names, with figures and dates. They were written with varying degrees of legibility, and many were no signatures at all, but crosses and notations, such as, "John Waterman (X) His Mark."

"Sign below, 'ere," ordered Jarvis, pointing to a space near the foot of one of the sheets.

Jim took the pen but hesitated. "Do you—are you sure we're leaving right away?" he asked.

"We'll be castin' off inside of 'arf an hour," the mate replied. Then he laughed harshly as he read the boy's thoughts. "No fear," he said. "Nobody'll see this afore we sail. Ye can sign yer own name, quite safe."

Jim reddened and wrote down his name with a flourish of finality. Jarvis watched him with an amused smile. "The pay," he said, "in case ye were in too much of an 'urry to notice, is six dollars a month, payable if an' when the vessel returns to its 'ome port."

The smile vanished from his mean mouth. "Now make yerself busy till we're clear," he snapped. "Clean out yer bunk fer a starter. Old Cato used it last, an' 'e was none too particular."

As he departed up the companion Jim had a vivid recollection of Ben Derry's words about cockney mates.

There was a narrow bunk tucked away under a sort of cupboard at the port side of the passage. Jim cleaned it out as best he could, ridding it of the heap of smelly rags that he found there and getting down to an old straw tick at the bottom. On this he spread the blanket and sat down to wait.

From the deck came noises—the rhythmic thud of coiling rope, the squeal of a block, and an occasional gruff voice. But he heard no singing or laughter—none of the jubilation he had imagined as prevailing on a ship about to sail.

There was something strange about the *White Angel.* He felt it—a vague uneasiness that came from no single cause. Perhaps, he thought, trying to reassure himself, it was simply his ignorance. He ought to be glad that his adventure was moving so smoothly. A berth on a ship ready for sea, and bound for the tropics! He was in luck!

Just then he heard a sound outside that brought him suddenly to his feet. It was his father's voice.

"They told me he was seen coming this way," Jonathan Slater was saying. "A strong lad, well grown. You're sure he might not have stolen aboard here?" There was an anxious note in his deep voice that brought a catch in Jim's throat. In another instant he would have sprung up the companion. But Jarvis was answering now.

"No, sir, 'e couldn't possibly 'ave been 'ere, for I've been standin' at this very spot since noon."

Jim's father seemed to be hesitating. "Well," he said finally, "I'll seek him further, then. But if he shows up here, send the boy home. He's but a green country lad an' knows nought o' the sea. He'd never make a sailor."

As he heard, Jim flushed red and slowly sat down once more.

Five minutes later Captain Hack came out of the cabin and climbed the companion without a glance at the boy in the corner. He was not as tall a man as Jim had thought him, but hard and rugged as a gnarled old oak. When he walked it could be seen that one of his legs was shorter than the other. He moved slowly, painfully, planting his feet with a rolling limp, and giving a little grunt at every step.

From the deck his voice sounded in a sharp-spoken order, the words of which the boy did not catch. Feet thudded on the planking, forward, and there was a creaking noise from the windlass. Then Jim felt the ship stir. They were warping her out of her moorings.

III

 SMALL porthole admitted light to the starboard side of the companion passage, and from it Jim watched the schooner's progress. He had gathered from Jarvis' orders that he was not wanted on deck, and he was glad he did not have to show himself till they were safely away from the city.

Slowly, the vessel swung out into the narrow roadstead of the Providence River and, aided by the tide, soon left the wharf-lined water front. Through the afternoon Jim saw the brown shores of Narragansett Bay slip past and by sunset they were well down the coast of Prudence Island, moving steadily with a smart breeze abeam.

26

At a sound of feet at the head of the companionway, Jim left his porthole and went back to the bunk under the cuddy. Captain Hack came stumping down the steps, followed by Jarvis and a big man in a sea-cloak whom Jim had not seen before.

Jarvis stopped and beckoned to the boy. "Come 'ere," he said, "and be spry about it. The cap'n wants his supper." He waited long enough to show Jim where the pewter and plate were kept, and told him to go forward to the galley and fetch the meal. Then he followed the others into the cabin.

Following his directions, Jim hastily laid four places on the cabin table, then took a big brass tray and set out in search of the galley. One of the sailors gave him a contemptuous look when he asked how to reach it. "Follow yer nose!" he told the boy, and jerked a thumb in the direction of the foremast.

As he went forward Jim realized that the advice was more practical than it had sounded. Savory odors were coming from the doorway of a low structure nestling just under the jaws of the fore-boom. His nose should have given him ample guidance. As he pushed the door farther open he almost ran into a swarthy, bearded man, thick-set and ferocious-looking. It was the Portuguese cook. Huge silver earrings gleamed in his black hair, and in his waistband he carried a shining knife at least eighteen inches long.

"Here!" he cried, scowling. "W'at you wan'—eh?"

Then he saw what it was Jim carried and he lost his truculence. With deft fingers he loaded meat and potatoes and bread on the tray, showed the boy how to balance it on one arm, and placed a steaming coffee pot in his other hand.

Hurrying back to the cabin, Jim proceeded to serve the men already seated at the table. It was a task in which he had had little experience, but he tried hard to cover up his awkwardness. If this was to be his introduction to a life on the bounding main, he would do his best and hope for something different later on.

At the captain's right hand sat the newcomer Jim had seen entering a few moments earlier. He was a huge, paunchy hulk of a fellow with a pock-mocked, dissipated face and little eyes that had purplish pouches under them. He was addressed as Mr. Creadon, and the boy knew enough of sea etiquette to gather from his position at the table that he was the first mate and Jarvis the second. Opposite them was the fourth member of the *White Angel's* afterguard—a man they called Dr. Brown when they spoke to him—evidently the ship's surgeon. He had a bony body and a long, cadaverous face. His nose was likewise long and sniffy, and he constantly plied it with snuff from an old silver snuff-box. He was dressed in sober landsman's clothes, and his expression was that of an austere dominie. But there was a network of tell-tale red veins about his cheekbones, and his hand shook as he lifted his glass.

There was little talk and no merriment among the diners. Jarvis went on deck as soon as he had finished eating, but the three others sat long around a demijohn of Jamaica rum. Jim cleared the table as best he could and fed himself from the remnants of the meal. Then he went to the cramped little bunk in the cuddy and curled up under his blanket. He was too tired to lie awake. The murmur of the sea and the soft creak of the ship's timbers lulled him soon to sleep. And though the sinister eyes and mirthless laughter of Jethro Hack haunted his dreams, he did not open his eyes till daybreak.

It was the big mate, Creadon, who woke him. Jim sat up, gasping, with half the breath knocked out of him, and saw the giant looming there in the dim light, the boot with which he had kicked him still resting on the side of the bunk.

"So-o," said the mate, "ye're the new cabin-boy, are ye?" He spoke with a sort of rasping purr and his eyes were half closed, like those of a cat that has found a disabled mouse. "An' I'm to make a sailor of ye, eh?" he went on. Then his lips drew back in a snarl. "Roll out here, ye big lummox!" he roared, and lifted a hand threateningly.

Jim jumped up with alacrity. "Ay, ay, sir!" he answered, in a voice that tried to sound seamanly.

Creadon gave a short laugh. "Rustle up the breakfast in a hurry," said he. "Then when ye've finished the cabin work, report to me on deck."

Jim found the weather had changed when he went forward to bring the breakfast from the galley. There was a chill, gray murk blowing up from the southeast, and the long seas marched to meet the schooner in sullen, lead-colored hills. No shore was visible now except a dark line in the haze to starboard.

Fascinated as he was by his first sight of the open ocean, the boy had no time for dillydallying. He hastened back to the cabin and waited first on Dr. Brown and Jarvis, then on Creadon and the captain. It was growing more and more difficult for him to keep his feet now, and once he spilled a plate of food when the ship pitched more sharply than usual. Jarvis was at the table when it happened, but he merely grinned sardonically at the boy's misfortune. "Better not let Cap'n Hack see yer do that!" he remarked.

Aside from measles and whooping-cough, Jim had never known an illness in his life. Perhaps the misery he felt during the next few hours was increased by this fact. His stomach became more and more uneasy as he worked, but he managed to finish serving the captain before disaster overtook him. At last, green and anguished, he staggered up the companion and across the deck to the lee bulwark, where he was desperately and forlornly sick.

While the boy was still hanging limply on the rail a heavy step sounded behind him. Creadon caught him by the shoulder and jerked him upright.

"Here, lubber," snapped the big mate, "quit playin'

baby! Show some backbone now, or I'll give ye reason to feel sick. Huh—chuckin' yer ballast with the water calm as a mill pond! What'll ye be doin' when we strike stormy weather off the Bermudas, eh?"

Jim stood up as straight as he was able. "All right, sir," he muttered weakly. "I'm feeling—pretty good again, now."

Creadon took him aft to the break of the poop. "Get a bucket an' a brush," he ordered. "We'll start ye right— scrubbin' the quarter-deck." And for the next four hours, under the critical eye of the mate, Jim labored unceasingly. Oddly enough, the violence of his seasickness abated when he got down on his hands and knees to work. And though he suffered a few qualms while serving the noon meal, he felt almost like himself again when he returned to the deck.

It was Jarvis who took him in hand for the afternoon. The schooner was running close-hauled and a grizzled old sailor spun the wheel, holding her nose into the heaving seas. The rat-eyed second mate lolled aft by the taffrail.

"I'll give yer a beginner's lesson in navigation," he remarked casually. "I don't suppose yer ever so much as 'eard o' boxin' the compass, eh?"

Jim straightened up. "Yes, sir," said he promptly. "Nor'—nor' by east—nor' nor'east—nor'east by nor'— nor'east—nor'east by east—" and so on through the rigmarole that Ben Derry, the carrier, had taught him long ago. Jarvis was quite evidently impressed. He gave a low whistle of surprise.

"Not bad, my bucko!" he said. Then his eyes narrowed. "An' could you bend a runnin' bowline?"

Jim shook his head. He thought it was some sort of sailor's knot, but beyond that his ideas were hazy. The mate cupped his hands and yelled forward. " 'Ere you, Matt Beckett," he called. "Take this lubber in charge an' teach 'im the knots. If 'e don't learn 'em sharp bring 'im back 'ere an' I'll give 'im knots aplenty on a rope's end."

A thin, yellow-visaged man with haggard eyes came shambling aft and Jim went to meet him.

"Come along o' me, boy," the fellow whispered hoarsely. "We'll snug down in the lee o' the fo'c's'le— out o' that wind." He shivered and pulled his reefer-jacket close around him. When they were settled he pulled a bit of spunyarn out of his pocket and proceeded to tie knots.

For the next hour there was little said. Beckett would tie the string slowly under Jim's intent gaze, then turn it over to the boy to imitate. "There," he would mutter, "that's a reef-knot," or "That's a sheepshank." When Jim had gone through the whole repertory and could not only tie the knots but name them without a mistake, the sailor took back his spunyarn and blew on his hands to warm them.

"Cold!" he whispered, looking strangely off to sea.

"I can't git it out o' my bones!" Then suddenly he turned his eyes on Jim, and the boy winced at the pain and horror that seemed to lie in their depths.

"Ye're a smart lad—a decent lad," said the seaman in that husky whisper of his. "Tell me—why, of all the ships that sail, did ye pick a craft like this to sign on?"

"I didn't have much choice," Jim grinned. "I was running away and this schooner was ready to sail. She's headed where I want to go, too—the tropics—the Ivory Coast—Africa!"

"*Africa!*" The whispered echo startled Jim with its bitterness. A ghastly look came over the sailor's face. "Ye mean," he said, "that ye didn't *know* what we was bound to Africa for?"

Jim stared at him and shook his head. "I don't know now," he answered.

The man cast a quick glance over his shoulder. "An' ye never before heard tell o' Jethro Hack—the hardest slave-cap'n that ever ran a load o' blacks out Calabar?"

Jim's mouth fell open in sudden astonishment. "Blacks!" he gasped. "Is the *White Angel* a slaver?"

His companion nodded. "One o' the devil's own ships," he muttered, and shivered violently. "I'm cold," he croaked, "—always cold. It's a curse on me fer what I saw once." Again he gave that furtive glance around, and then fixed Jim with his eye.

"I look old, boy, but I ain't," he said. "That's the devil's work, too. Six years back I was a spry young mate on a coastin' bark. Then one day in Havana I fell in with a smooth-spoke skipper named Homans, recruitin' hands fer a slave-runnin' v'yage in the brig *Brillante*. I'd never tried slavin', but I'd known a plenty o' seamen that looked on it as a godly trade. An' there was big money in the mate's share. So I j'ined. We made a quick trip over, an' loaded six hundred from the barracoons in Bonny River. Six hundred poor doomed souls—mostly boys an' gals!'' A shudder ran through him, but he continued.

"The second day out we sighted a cruiser. We crowded on sail an' give him the slip. But a day later he was after us again with three others to help. The blockade was mighty stiff, right then.

"When they were a couple of leagues off, the wind died. I'll never fergit that mornin'—the sea smooth as oil, an' the sky like a brass pot. Through the glasses Cap'n Homans saw 'em lower a whole fleet o' small-boats, an' he knew we hadn't a chance. But the treaty law was that a slaver could only be captured if she had slaves aboard her." He hesitated and shivered once more.

"The skipper gave an order to haul our biggest anchor-chain up through the hawse-hole an' run it clear 'round the ship on the deck outside the rail. Then we opened the hatches an' brought up the slaves from the hold an' we tied their leg-irons to the chain with short lengths o' rope—two blacks to every link."

The man was trembling so that he could hardly speak, and Jim felt a chill of horror as he listened.

"There was still no sign o' wind," Beckett whispered. "An' when the cruisers' boats were a mile away, Homans told me to let go the anchor. He had a pistol in his hand an'—I did it. They screamed, queer-like, as the chain slid off, an' all at once I was cold—cold as a dead man. I've never been warm since."

He paused, licking his dry lips. "Homans was a hard one," he went on after a moment. "When the officers hailed him, he stood there on the quarter-deck an' laughed at 'em like the fiend he was. The smell o' slaves was in the ship—the manacles an' whips lay 'round the decks—the big cook-kettles was simmerin' with food fer six hundred mouths. But there was no black soul aboard. They couldn't lay hands on us. We sailed back an' got a new cargo, an' made a profit on the v'yage. Hah!

"I tried other ships after that, but it was no use. The curse was on me an' I was never fit to be a mate again. Cold! Always cold! An' so I stick to slavers, 'cause they sail mostly in hot latitudes. Boy," he finished with a shake of his head, "I'm sorry fer ye!"

IV

HEN Jim got over the first shock of his discovery he went about his tasks aboard the *White Angel* with one determined thought in the back of his head. He must escape. How he was to do it was a question he could not answer yet, but his resolve was firm. Sooner or later he knew a chance would come. In the meantime he set himself to learn everything he could about the job of being a sailor—to pick up all the odds and ends of sea knowledge that came his way. He had a feeling that some day he might use them in getting clear of the slaver.

The boy took hold of his duties well. He could sense a grudging admission of this even in the attitude of the sneering cockney, Jarvis. Creadon bullied him when he was drunk, and ignored him in his sober moments. After a few savage reprimands the captain rarely spoke to him. Jim quickly learned his wants and peculiarities and performed his service accordingly. Yet even when the boy was doing the cabin tasks as punctiliously as a steward, he sometimes caught Hack's glance upon him, and saw that terrifying glint in the deep-set hawk eyes. At such times his hands would tremble in spite of him, and he was lucky if he did not spill the rum as he poured it.

Among the crew Jim made few friends. They were a sorry lot of rogues for the most part. Ten of the thirteen foremast hands were Spanish or West Indian—dirty, unkempt fellows, voluble enough in their own tongue, but scowling and sullen in the presence of Americans. Besides the haggard and ghost-ridden Matt Beckett there was a solemn little ship's carpenter from Martha's Vine-yard, and a hard-bitten old man called Johnny Buck, who wore great white mustaches and had once been a wrecker on the Florida Keys.

It was from this trio that Jim learned most of his sea-lore, and drew the only real companionship he knew aboard the slaver. There was also the bo's'n—a sour-faced Cape Cod man with a fringe of chin-whiskers— and Manuel, the cook, whose forbidding appearance caused the lad to keep his distance.

The heavy weather they had encountered the second day of the voyage was over in forty-eight hours. After that, as they sailed south, the air stayed brisk and cold, but fair winds favored them. At the end of a week they passed Cape Hatteras and nosed out into the balmy weather of the Gulf Stream.

Working and loafing through the long, bright days,

Jim gained a deal of information from his three friends forward. One thing he found out was that the schooner was heading for Cuba, in order to take aboard supplies and add to the crew.

"There's allus a lot o' sots an' cutthroats hangin' around them island ports," Johnny Buck, the old wrecker, told him. "The slavers buy 'em from the crimps, ashore, an' throw 'em below on the ballast till they're sober. They got me thataway more'n once. Knocked me in the head with a capstan-bar, an' when I come to, there I was on my way to the Congo."

The tough old sinner had started life as a fisherman and beachcomber, he told Jim. But he had soon given that up for the more lucrative trade of robbing wrecks. And for forty years, with occasional excursions into smuggling, slave-running, and piracy, he had followed his calling all up and down the Caribbean.

"The wreckin' business is crowded, now," he said, "an' I'm gittin' too old to fight fer my rights. But I lost the power o' smell a while back, an' so I don't mind the slave-trade like I might." He winked at Jim. "A sharp nose ain't no advantage whatsomever aboard a blackbirder," he concluded.

The carpenter was the handy man of the ship. He could make anything that was needed with the simple tools he had at hand. A great part of his work was really not carpentry at all but blacksmithing. Jim spent hours with him at his little forge, where he fashioned and repaired the leg-irons that would come into use when the cargo was shipped. Sometimes the boy accompanied him to the slave-holds under the main deck. He was astonished to find so little headroom that he had to crawl on hands and knees. Nowhere in the whole dark space was the deck more than thirty inches above the floor. A foul, stale odor still clung to the place. The main hold was about twenty feet wide by forty in length. "They'll pack two hundred full-grown bucks in here," said the little man with a chuckle. "Ye'd never believe it till ye've seen it done."

Matt Beckett was rarely willing to talk. He huddled, shivering, in the lee of the fo'c's'le, even now that they were enjoying summer weather. But when the mood was on him he could tell the boy more about ships and rigging and navigation than any other man aboard.

There came a morning when Jim woke in his bunk before daylight with a strange sensation. For a moment he sat rubbing his eyes, unable to discover what it was that seemed different. Then it came to him that there was scarcely any motion to the schooner. The heaving pitch and roll of the open sea was gone, and in its place he felt only a gentle rocking. Forward he could hear a rumble of chains and the sound of short-spoken orders.

Jim slipped into his shirt and trousers and went on deck. In the soft light of dawn he made out a green coast fringed with tropical trees, and the breeze brought him a scent of heavy-odored blossoms. He drew a deep breath and looked eagerly about him at the harbor. The schooner lay at anchor a mile from the nearest shore, and the land reached around her in a deep horseshoe. Three or four other ships of various rigs were moored a little distance away, and close to the water's edge stretched a low white town like a broken string of beads.

Jarvis must have seen the look of excitement on the boy's face, for as he passed him he stopped and spoke. "No, me lad, ye don't get off the ship today," he said with a mean little grin. "Step smart below now, an' lay out the breakfast. The skipper'll be up early."

Under the watchful eye of the second mate Jim spent the morning at odd jobs of scrubbing and polishing. He looked enviously after the longboat when it went ashore at noon, and measured the distance to land with his eye once more. He was a good swimmer, and he believed he could make it if he had a way of leaving the vessel unobserved. He was assigned to no watch because of his cabin duties. Perhaps if he waited for darkness, a chance would offer.

The afternoon dragged slowly. About an hour before sunset the boat returned, loaded almost to the gunwale with bags and barrels of provisions. At dusk she put off again, and this time Captain Hack was sitting in the stern-sheets.

"He's goin' to shanghai a crew," Beckett told Jim as they watched the rowers pull away. "That's the last job to be done before we start our v'yage. The food an' water's all stowed, an' the trade goods. That was what we put into Providence fer—cotton cloth an' beads an' such. Soon as he's collected half a dozen more hands we'll weigh anchor."

Creadon had the first watch, and he set the men to preparing the schooner for departure. By the time it was fully dark she lay under riding-lights, hove short on her anchor and ready to sail. Jim waited till the deck amidships was empty and the mate was looking off astern. Then he darted forward and hid himself in a coil of rope by the foot of the foremast. He was barefooted and clad only in duck trousers and a cotton shirt. These he knew he could take off in the water if they hampered his swimming.

He waited, hoping Creadon would step below for a drink, as he sometimes did. What he wanted was a chance to slide quietly over the rail in the dark. But his plan was suddenly ruined. The mate came clumping forward and called one of the sailors.

"Here," he ordered, "hang a lantern in the larboard shrouds, so the boat can see to come alongside. I heard the noise o' their oars a minute ago."

At his direction a bright light was placed in the ratlines right opposite Jim's place of concealment. All he could do now was cower down inside his low wall of tarry hemp and hope to escape discovery. In this at least he was lucky, for when, a moment later, the longboat came scraping along the schooner's planks, all of the watch on deck came running to help at the falls. And in the confusion Jim was able to step out of his hiding-place and join the group, unnoticed.

In the little circle of light shed by the swaying lantern five men were passed up over the rail. All of them were ragged and unkempt, and the first three were either drugged or so far gone in liquor that they sprawled on the deck unconscious. The fourth man was awake and ugly. He started to shout something angrily and was promptly knocked down by a blow of Creadon's heavy fist.

As the last of the five was lifted aboard, Jim heard a chuckle from the bo's'n, below in the longboat. "Handle this one careful," he called. "We may need him later. He's s'posed to be a gunner."

Without ceremony the newcomers were bundled into the fo'c'sle and the boat was swung to the deck. Within thirty minutes the anchor had been catted and the *White Angel* was standing out through the harbor mouth, her big sails drawing in the steady night breeze.

Jim waited, hoping for another chance to go over the side, but the full watch was on deck and he knew he would be seen. At last, with a regretful look toward the fading shore-line, he went below. He was Africa-bound now, and there was no way out of it.

For two days the schooner skirted the Cuban coast, and several times in the week that followed, Jim sighted the far-off peaks of mountainous islands. Then all land was left behind as they forged steadily east by south. Much as the boy hated the idea of being aboard a slaver, he could not help enjoying the voyage. The wind held and the sun shone, day after day. Only once, in mid-Atlantic, did they encounter bad weather, and then for two days the ship ran under a storm jib before a westerly gale that drove her on her course.

On fair days Jim would lie out along the bowsprit or cling to the fore-chains and watch the clear green water curl into spray under the vessel's prow. There he got his first view of flying fish and the dolphins that played along in the path of the ship.

Sometimes they ran past patches of drifting Sargasso weed. Then the sailors would whisper vague tales of that mysterious sea where the derelict hulks of missing ships were said to ride together in a gruesome fleet, locked fast in the weed's grip.

A little flock of seabirds came after the schooner. Sometimes several of them at once would settle in the rigging and teeter there, flapping wide wings and screaming shrilly. Each morning when the cook threw overboard a tubful of waste from the galley, the hungry birds flew down from their perches. Fluttering and squawking, they would settle on the water and fight for the scraps till the ship had left them far astern.

There came a bright forenoon when Jim arrived on deck to find the air filled with clamor and the sky dark with wheeling wings. He went aft to old Johnny Buck, who was handling the helm, and asked him where so many gulls had come from.

"Ho, them?" said the old wrecker. "They're visitors from shore. Keep yer eye peeled over the port bow this evenin' an' ye'll see land—the Cape Verde Islands."

The veteran sailor knew what he was talking about. Just at sunset Jim saw a dim peak rise out of the haze on the eastern horizon. They had crossed the Atlantic. Before them stood the outposts of Africa!

The schooner changed her course that night and ran southerly with a spanking breeze behind her. When Jim had cleared the cabin table after supper, he saw the skipper spread a chart on the worn oak and bend over it in conference with his first mate. What they were discussing he could not tell, but several times he caught the names of ports—Bangalang, Rio Pongo, Calabar, and others he had never heard of before. Names with strange, savage syllables that set the boy's nerves tingling.

It was four days before they sighted land again. Then one morning Jim came on deck to fetch the breakfast and found the schooner hove-to off a low wooded shore, half seen through silver mists. A heavy smell of decaying vegetation was in the air. Near the galley door he encountered Matt Beckett.

"Is it the Ivory Coast?" Jim blurted eagerly.

The yellow-visaged sailor shook his head. "Naw, we ain't goin' that far, this trip. We're on the Windward Coast, somewheres below Sierra Leone, I reckon. There's

HE SAW THE SKIPPER SPREAD A CHART ON THE
WORN OAK

a new tradin' station—Gallinas—that the cap'n's been talkin' about. Shouldn't wonder if this is it. Looks like a rummy sort o' place, don't it? An' cold!" he added with his eternal shiver.

Jim found it anything but cold when the sun had burned the mist away. It was a windless day, and vaporous waves of heat seemed to radiate from the low islands, rank with reeds and mangroves. In front of them stretched a bar on which the waves broke in a long line of white.

A seaman had been sent aloft, and now half a dozen brightly colored signal flags were broken out from the fore-peak. All hands were above decks and watching the shore intently. After ten or fifteen minutes a faint hail came from the nearest island, and they saw a naked negro launch a canoe and paddle swiftly toward them. He shot his craft through the cresting breakers of the bar, then rested his paddle a moment and studied the ship, shading his eyes with one hand. At last, apparently satisfied that she was not a cruiser in disguise, he drove the canoe alongside.

"That's the Krooman pilot," remarked old Johnny Buck, "comin' to take us in. We'll stretch our legs on dry ground tonight."

V

T FIVE o'clock that afternoon—"two bells in the first dog watch," as he had learned to call it—Jim Slater stood on the beach and looked about him at the continent of his dreams. He had come ashore in the longboat with the watering party, and now he had a few moments' respite while the first boatload of water barrels was being rowed aboard.

Gallinas was like many another of the slave-stations that dotted the Guinea Coast all the way from Gambia to Calabar. It lay at the mouth of a slow-flowing tidal river among low, marshy islands overgrown with a matted jungle of cane and mangrove forests. Moist, sweltering heat hung over it, and droning swarms of mosquitoes filled the air. Nothing but the expectation of rich profits would have lured white men to such a place.

On the swampy mainland stood the factor's house, its thatched roof and broad verandas sheltered from the sun by thick-growing clumps of trees. A village of friendly natives straggled up-river beyond the factory and ended with a high-peaked conical hut—the dwelling of the black chief. The slave barracoons were placed on several of the nearer islands. They were huge stockades of hardwood posts driven deep into the ground and lashed with iron. Roofs of light poles and grass thatch covered them. Anywhere from a hundred to five hundred negroes could be crowded into each of these inclosures and kept there until a slaver called for a cargo.

Securing slaves from the interior was never a very difficult matter. The coast trader made it his business always to maintain friendly relations with the more powerful chiefs of the up-river country. Tribes and villages were constantly at war with each other, and for centuries it had been the custom for the victors to make slaves of their conquered enemies. Sometimes the entire population of a village would be captured and shipped down the stream in canoes. When they reached the coast the victorious chiefs would bargain with the trader until they obtained a satisfactory price for their captives and then return laden with rum, powder, muskets, cotton cloth, and other trade goods, ready to wage another war.

To Gallinas, the year before, had come Don Pedro Blanco, a young Spanish adventurer who was destined to become the richest and most powerful of all the African slave-dealers. In spite of the fact that the slave-traffic had been outlawed by all the principal European nations and by the United States for more than a decade, the smuggling of blacks continued a paying business. British cruisers constantly patrolled the coast, but hundreds of slave-ships ran the gauntlet every season. Don Pedro secured his negroes for perhaps twenty dollars a head, and the price paid him by the slave-captains averaged at least double that amount. They in turn were often able to sell the blacks in Cuba or South America for as high as four hundred dollars apiece.

Jim had a glimpse of the young Spaniard, three or four days later, when Captain Hack invited him aboard the schooner to settle the terms of his purchase. He arrived in a barge of state, rowed by ten picked negroes, and mounted the ladder with as much formality as an admiral of the fleet. He was a slim, dark, handsome fellow with somber eyes. His immaculate clothes and graceful manners would have done credit to a courtier. And though he spoke English with some difficulty, his voice was low-pitched and musical.

Wearing a clean suit of white duck, donned for the occasion, Jim waited on the table. Manuel had outdone himself in preparing a meal, and the regular viands of the ship's larder were augmented by chickens and fresh vegetables from the shore. When the repast was over Don Pedro smiled at Jim and complimented the Yankee skipper on his cabin-boy.

"W'en you dine weeth me at Casa Blanco, breeng heem, too," said the trader, and Hack, mellowed by his third noggin of rum, agreed that he would. So it came about that Jim had a chance, two days after, to see the interior of the slave factory—a privilege that few ordinary seamen ever enjoyed.

Just before dusk the *White Angel's* party landed from the gig at a flimsy dock on the riverside and walked up a path of white sand to the house. The trader's dwelling, although large and spacious, was built of bamboo, wattled with mud in the native fashion. At the wide doorway they were met by a mulatto boy in full butler's regalia and ushered into the reception hall. It was a cheerful room, tastefully furnished with rugs, chairs and tables brought from Spain.

Don Pedro came forward to meet them, extending a hand in greeting. "Welcome, Señors!" said he, and bade them be seated. After a few minutes a second black servant entered, salaamed deeply, and announced dinner.

Captain Hack, Dr. Brown, the surgeon, and Creadon, the first mate, were shown to places at the large center table with their host. Jim, owing to his rank, was served at a smaller table by the wall. An amazing quantity of food was set before him—native dishes, cooked and brought on in calabashes, huge leaves, and other strange utensils. Evidently Don Pedro wanted to give them a taste of true African fare.

These foods were, for the most part, unsavory-looking and queer-smelling, though some of them were delicious when he tried them. There was rice and young bamboo shoots with a dark sauce, a sort of stew of ground-nuts and herbs, and another thick, viscous mess which Jim could not even bring himself to taste. He had heard too many tales from the sailors about native delicacies made from toads, lizards, and serpents. Finally a juicy brown roast of mutton was brought on and Jim was able to make an excellent meal.

After the older men had finished their wine and lighted Blanco's Havana cigars, the party adjourned to one of the verandas. The trader suggested that they visit the barracoons and look over some slaves recently brought in. Accordingly torches were lighted and the barge of state was manned by Don Pedro's strapping crew. In a few moments the party landed on the nearest of the prison islands.

Two white guards armed with muskets stood before the entrance of the big stockade. They saluted their employer in military fashion, and at his command opened a narrow wicket gate leading into the inclosure.

There had been a murmur of guttural voices from the barracoon as they approached, but now these suddenly fell still. Jim followed the others through the wicket and looked about him, straining his eyes into the dark. At first he could see nothing, and the only noise in the place was a hushed sound of breathing. Then one of the trader's men stepped forward with a whip in his right hand and a torch held high in his left. He shouted something in a native dialect, and Jim saw the massed shadows at the rear of the stockade break and sway. Here and there a naked black body caught the light with a dull gleam. It was like the slow writhing of a tangle of black-snakes in a cave.

The overseer cracked his whip impatiently and the negroes came on, to the edge of the lighted area. They were all bucks—upwards of a hundred and fifty of them —big-boned, black-skinned men from the deep jungle. Their rolling eyes looked uneasy and frightened.

"Wild as a bunch o' buffaloes!" growled Captain Hack.

Don Pedro nodded. They were from the interior, he explained. A fighting tribe captured by a ruse and traded five or six hundred miles across country. But they were strong—built for work in the cotton and cane fields. They would bring good prices in Louisiana. "Look at their chief," he said, "the vera beeg one, standing behind."

Jim caught a glimpse of an ebony giant with a haughty face, who loomed head and shoulders above the others.

"Hunh!" the skipper grunted. "I've got no use for them Congo kings. Shipped one once in Calabar an' had nothin' but trouble out o' him. Had to shoot him 'fore we landed."

The trader smiled politely. "But thees one will not make trouble," he replied. "He has a wife and child in the women's barracoon."

The visitors moved on to another island, where they saw an entirely different sort of spectacle. This stockade was filled with coast negroes of mixed races who seemed quite contented with their lot. They grimaced and showed off before the white men. Some chattered and sang. Others danced to the throbbing beat of a tom-tom.

Don Pedro strolled among them, calling the captain's attention to particularly "likely-looking" slaves. This one, he said, would make a good house boy. That one was experienced with cattle. And though Hack maintained the noncommittal attitude expected of a buyer, Jim could see that he was satisfied with the exhibit.

Half an hour after their return to the mainland, goodnights were said, and the Americans rowed back to the schooner.

It was nearly a week before the *White Angel* was ready for sea. Slave provender, in the shape of rice and vegetables, had to be stowed aboard, and there was some dickering over the price of the blacks and the quality of Hack's trade goods. At last everything was settled. Native scouts, sent out in boats, reported the coast clear of cruisers. All that remained was to ship the slaves. For a whole day the negroes were coming aboard, a score at a time, from big canoes paddled alongside the schooner. On deck the crew took the males and fettered them in pairs, ankle to ankle, then drove them below to take their places in the slave deck. They were laid in rows on the planking, each on his right side, so as to allow the blood to circulate more freely. Their knees were bent and every man lay with his back against his neighbor's stomach. This packing was done methodically, even to placing the tallest slaves in the waist of the ship, where the hold was a foot or two broader than forward.

The women and children were not put in irons, but their quarters—aft, under the cabin—were even tighter and worse ventilated than the men's.

By sunset the tally was complete. Four hundred and ninety blacks lay sandwiched, "spoon-fashion," in the bowels of the schooner.

The *White Angel* weighed anchor and sailed across Gallinas bar on the crest of a flood tide. And before the moon was well risen she was beating out to sea against a light westerly breeze. The dreaded "middle passage" had begun.

Jim, glad of their departure from the stifling malarial heat of the Guinea Coast, stole on deck that night for a breath of cool air. It was good to be at sea again—to feel the slow lurch of the vessel and hear the creak of taut cordage.

Matt Beckett was alone at the wheel, and the boy

joined him there. "It's a fine night," he suggested, with the idea of making conversation. The sailor said nothing for a while. His gaunt face was set to the west, and he humored the wheel with the deft familiarity of years. Then he turned his hollow eyes on Jim with that strange look that the boy had come to fear.

"It's an ill-starred v'yage," he whispered. "I don't say what'll happen, but no good is comin' to us. Listen!"

Jim stood breathless, trying to catch a sound. At first he heard only the wind in the shrouds and the groaning of timbers. Finally another noise came to him—a muffled moan of inexpressible terror and sadness. It rose slowly to a wail, gathering the strength of many voices, then died away once more in silence.

"The niggers," breathed Beckett. "They know. I never heard that moanin' at the start of a v'yage but once before. That was on Bloody Homans' brig. It'll come sooner or later. Mebbe the plague—mebbe some other kind o' trouble—but it'll git us. You wait an' see!"

Daylight drove the fear of Beckett's words out of Jim's head. The wind held, the sun shone, and the crew went cheerfully about their tasks. Even the dour captain seemed for once to be in a good humor. So they sailed for a week and logged close on twelve hundred miles. "At this gait," the boy heard Jarvis say, "we'll be on the Gulf coast in a month."

But the luck did not hold. On the tenth day out they ran into a storm that carried them many leagues to the southward. After that the wind was fitful for a week, and then it died altogether. The schooner drifted aimlessly day after day with sagging sails. Tempers grew short. Creadon spent more time than usual over his grog in the cabin, and when he came on deck he was always ugly, ready to bully the first seaman who crossed his path.

The slaves were brought up for exercise each morning, and on days when Dr. Brown was sober he looked them over carefully for signs of disease. He was a strange, melancholy man, extraordinarily skillful at his craft. Jim heard it said more than once that he had been a famous surgeon in Philadelphia until the liquor he drank had ruined him. At least his medicine seemed effective among the crowded blacks. So far only half a dozen had died, and Jim wondered at this, for the sickening stench of the slave-decks had become almost unbearable.

Matt Beckett was the only soul on the ship who got any enjoyment out of being becalmed. The terrific heat was to his liking, and he took a sort of morose pleasure in seeing his prophecies of bad luck coming true. "But this ain't all," he murmured to Jim. "This is only the beginnin'. Mark my words."

At last they caught a breeze and began to make headway again. Captain Hack crowded all sail on the ship and drove her night and day, for time was vital now. Jim heard rumors among the men. Some of the water

casks in the hold had sprung leaks, and the supply would
soon be running low.

They were eight weeks out when they sighted the
Cuban coast, and Hack would have landed there to re-
plenish his stores, but a threatening sail appeared astern
and followed them for the best part of two days. So they
pressed on into the Gulf. And the boy began to take
heart, for he had a feeling now that his chance to leave
the *White Angel* was drawing closer.

VI

HE long, shrill chirp of the bo's'n's whistle broke strangely into the heavy hush of afternoon. Jim heard it and rose from the bunk where he had sat drowsily polishing the captain's pewter. As he listened there was a thud of bare feet along the deck, forward, and a series of sharp commands in the barking voice of Creadon, the mate. Then, from somewhere far off, came the unmistakable dull boom of a cannon.

It was the first time Jim had heard that sound at sea, but a shiver of excitement went through him, for he knew what it was. Breathless, he stood a moment listening, then dropped the pewter plates in the cuddy and ran up the companionway.

Most of the crew were clustered around the swivel gun, mounted aft. Three or four were busy removing the tarpaulin that usually covered it. Others rolled up round-shot and kegs of powder. In the bustle and confusion only the gnarled, stooping figure of the captain stood motionless beside the wheel. It was at that moment that he caught sight of Jim. The boy saw his eyes glint and heard the roar of his hard voice.

"Here, you lubber," Hack bawled, "cut below and fetch your blanket!"

As he hastened to obey, Jim heard the sound of the distant cannon a second time, and a third report followed close. Stripping the cover from his berth, he returned to the deck, and there, under Creadon's orders, he drew a bucket of sea water and soused the blanket till it was drenching wet.

"Now then," growled the mate, "stand by this powder and put out anything that looks like a spark."

For the first time Jim had a chance to look around him. The wind had dropped again, and an ominous silence had settled over the deck. The crew for the most part crouched by the bulwark, staring off to the south, where a white sail stood above the polished sea. At grimly regular intervals a puff of smoke would blossom from the low gray hull of the stranger, and seconds later would come the hollow *boom* of the report.

No air stirred. The schooner rolled slowly to the lazy Gulf swell, and overhead the great sails hung limp. Heat beat down on them from a sky like a furnace. Yet there must have been some current of breeze to the southward, for the other ship seemed to be coming nearer.

Jim heard the seamen talking in undertones. The man nearest him, Johnny Buck, the weather-beaten old wrecker from the Florida Keys, pointed a scarred hand toward the enemy. "Navy cutter," he murmured. "See her flags? But ol' Hack'll never give in now, when he's this close to the bayous. He'd beach her first."

"Can't beach her 'thout a breeze," answered the bo's'n. "Give us half a hatful o' wind an' we could walk off. But that feller's makin' way an' he means business. 'Twon't be long 'fore he gits our range."

Jim's knees sagged and he felt a wave of nausea sweep him. It wasn't fear nor seasickness. It wasn't even the foul smell of the ship, for he had become hardened to that. What had struck him was a sudden bitter sense of shame. All his life he had dreamed of fighting for his country. He had visioned himself on the deck of a Yankee frigate, standing to his guns and battling valiantly— dying, if need be, for a piece of starry bunting.

There was the flag. He could see the brave flutter of its colors at the cutter's masthead. And here was he, thanks to his own folly, aboard a filthy slaver. Cabin-boy of Jethro Hack's *White Angel*, sixty days out from Gallinas, with a contraband cargo of Africans under her hatches and a lying Portuguese flag at her main-truck— now about to be sent to the bottom as a public enemy. And much glory, thought Jim, would there be in that!

The naval craft's cannon sounded again and a round shot came skipping over the water, barely missing the schooner's bowsprit. Captain Hack raged at the sight.

"Are ye loaded, Mister?" he bellowed, and to the mate's affirmative reply, "Then let 'em have it!"

But the six-pounder swivel gun was too light a piece for the range, and they saw a splash of spray where the shot landed, far to leeward of the cutter.

At that moment there came a hail from the lookout in the cross-trees.

"There's a bit o' breeze comin' on the port quarter," he shouted. All strained their eyes to the south and saw there, sure enough, a darker streak along the water. It reached the cutter and she bowed closer with filling canvas.

Swiftly the line of wind advanced, and there was sudden action on the slaver's deck while her crew made ready for it. The cordage creaked as the first puff came over, and then the huge, dirty sails began to draw. With a sort of slatternly grace the big schooner leaned to leeward and gathered speed. It was none too soon, for at the next shot from the cutter there was a splintering crash aft. The *White Angel* yawed, then steadied and came back on her course. Part of the rudder had been shot away.

On the next attempt, however, the cutter's missile fell astern, and gradually the slim, long hull of the slave ship pulled ahead, till the sail of the pursuing craft was a tiny dot in the haze of the horizon. Fast as she was sailing, Captain Hack looked aloft with a dissatisfied scowl. At length he called the mate aft. "Mr. Creadon," he said, "this breeze won't hold. We must make all the

A ROUND SHOT CAME SKIPPING OVER THE WATER, BARELY
MISSING THE SCHOONER'S BOWSPRIT

northing we can, while it lasts. Break out those spare tops'ls, an' bend 'em on."

From the sail locker was produced a pair of huge racing topsails, beautifully white, in contrast to the dingy gray of the regular canvas. Hastily the new sails were set, replacing the old ones, and the schooner lurched forward at a giddy pace, her lofty topmasts bending. Not until he had seen the last rope made fast and the white water rushing by under the schooner's lee did the captain stir from his post beside the wheel. He moved slowly, painfully, his rolling limp exaggerated by the swaying of the deck. As he passed Jim he glanced at the sun, now nearly set.

"Bring my supper, boy," he said, and descended the companion.

Jim got his brass tray from the cuddy and went forward. In the galley Manuel, bearded and scowling, was stirring one of the four huge kettles where the rice and yams and horse-beans were cooked for the slaves.

The cabin meal was ready, and Jim, loading his tray with platters, started aft. Dusk had fallen purple across the Gulf, and the breeze still sang in the taut shrouds. The boy turned his face to windward, drinking in grateful breaths of cool, untainted air. Then, from the bowels of the ship, came a sound that made him shudder. It was a murmur, hardly audible at first, that rose and gathered volume till its wailing minor chords vibrated in the deck timbers, then faded slowly to a broken moaning. There

was such dark agony in that long, muffled cry as chilled
Jim to the marrow of his bones. He had made his way as
far as the companion when he saw one of the crew move
over to the main hatch in leisurely fashion and throw off
a tarpaulin that had covered the grating during the fight
with the cutter.

"Belay there, ye black sons o' Ham," bellowed the
seaman, and spat deliberately between the bars.

As Jim's stumbling feet carried him down the stairs,
the last echo of misery from the slave deck was drowned
by a bull roar of laughter and a crash of tankards. In the
middle of the cabin table he saw the familiar straw-
covered jug of Jamaica rum, and gathered around it the
officers of the ship.

The captain interrupted his mirth long enough to de-
liver a tremendous oath. "Well, boy," he shouted,
"what's been keeping ye? These gentlemen are hungry.
Maybe it's a taste o' the cat ye need. I'll warrant Mr.
Creadon'll be glad to see to it."

Jim knew better than to open his mouth. With silent
haste he set the plates of food on the table and ran to
the cupboard for knives and forks. Then, before another
broadside could be delivered, he caught up the jug and
went from place to place, refilling the pewter tankards.
Hard experience had taught him that this was the safest
way to divert attention from himself. The men fell to,
then, without more words, and Jim went to crouch in a

corner, where he could remain as inconspicuous as possible.

From this vantage-point the boy watched the captain, ready to jump at his first command. Jethro Hack glanced from one to another of his officers as he ate. His mad, restless eyes burned deep in a face the color of old leather. He had taken off the mangy fur cap he wore on deck in all weathers, and his bare head showed a jagged scar at the temple, laid open long ago by some mutineer's belaying-pin. The crew said the pain in his leg made him cruel—that he drank to escape it. But drunk or sober, Jim knew he was dangerous.

Tonight he showed a bitter sort of humor, joked boisterously, bared his teeth in snarling laughter. The voyage was nearly over, and the wretched blacks he had bought from Don Pedro at Gallinas would soon be sold for a dozen times their cost—those that were left. The water was getting low, and they had had to throw too many bodies overboard of late. Jim heard him speak of the matter to the first mate after Jarvis had gone on deck.

"Beginning tomorrow," he said, "cut down their water rations. A pint for the big bucks, but half o' that for the wenches an' young uns. Blast it, Doctor"—he turned explosively to the surgeon—"can't you dig up some physic that'll stop their confounded thirst?"

"Hard to do, Cap'n, hard to do," drawled the doctor's

sardonic voice. "I might stop the beggars' thirst, but I'd likely stop their breathing at the same time."

"Well," Hack answered, "two more days o' fair wind should see us safe in the bayous. I don't reckon that pesky cutter'll come up with us again."

To Jim, sitting there in the shadow, the words held out a promise of hope. Two more days! He'd get away somehow—anyhow—once they came to anchor. Leave this ghastly ship forever—

"Boy!"

The captain poured himself a final drink and rose unsteadily. "Boy," he repeated, "clear away here, then get yourself off."

Jim stood up quickly. "Ay, ay, sir," he said, and went about it. Ten minutes later he left the cabin for his narrow bunk in the companion cuddy. Such air as reached him there was heavy with the fetid odor of the ship.

"Ugh!" he thought as he stretched on the bunk. "It's a wonder we're not *all* dead men aboard here. Sleep? I'll never get to sleep tonight!"

But Jim was tired. Almost before the thought had time to pass through his head his eyes had closed and he had slipped into welcome forgetfulness.

VII

IM was roused out at the crack of dawn to wait on Jarvis at his breakfast. The second mate looked glum as he sat down to the meal. Ordinarily he was given to ordering Jim about with a show of arrogance, but this morning he took no notice of him.

When Creadon came lumbering from his bunk, the junior officer's preoccupation was explained.

"The blacks are restless," he told the first mate. "Yellin' and gibberin' for water. Three more died in the night, and one tried to bite the bo's'n's leg when he went below to quiet 'em."

"That's to be expected," rumbled Creadon. "They're allus bad at the end o' the v'yage. We'll settle that with the whip. An' we ought to land 'em in two more days."

The morning was half gone before Jim finished his duties about the cabin. When at length he was free to go on deck he found the schooner riding with slack sails once more, under a hot and cloudless sky. They had completely outdistanced the cutter in the night, and no sail showed on the horizon. To the northward, however, along the shimmering border of sky and sea, there seemed to Jim to be a faint, dark line. Was it island or coast? Undoubtedly some of the sailors could tell him, but he dared not appear too eager.

After a few moments he strolled to the rail where the old Florida beachcomber leaned. As casually as possible he pointed to the north. "What land do you figure that is, Johnny?" he asked.

The wrecker squinted at the horizon. "Oh, the Mississippi shore, I reckon," he answered. "That or the Delta above the Balize."

The mainland! Jim's heart-beat quickened as he heard. And it could hardly be more than five or six leagues away. He made for his favorite retreat, the fore-chains—the one part of the schooner where he could momentarily forget his surroundings. Letting his legs down over the bows, he seated himself in a loop of the great cable that hung from the catted anchor. Just above him swelled the cracked wooden bosom of the angel that was the slave-ship's quaintly inappropriate figurehead. Six feet below him rolled the blue Gulf swell. Here he could sit, away from the sight of the deck and the scents of the hold, and watch the vivid ocean life that moved beneath him.

The sea swarmed with fish of every size and hue. There would be a sudden gleaming line of ripples alongside and a school of flying-fish would burst from the water, spread their kitelike fins, and go sailing for many yards above the surface. After them, following at breathless speed, would come the dolphins, cutting the water in long, leaping curves, their graceful bodies shining like burnished gold in the sun. They caught their prey sometimes in mid-air, sometimes just as the tired flying-fish returned to the water.

Other sea-rovers even larger than the dolphins made an occasional appearance. Twice Jim saw the jigging fin of a great gray shark moving lazily in the shadow of the sails. And once a dolphin, in the very act of seizing a flying-fish, was bitten almost in two by the savage teeth of a barracuda.

These hours spent in the fore-chains were more nearly happy than any he had known in all the long months of the westward voyage. They gave him his one respite from the grim horrors of life aboard the slaver. For he still loved the sea. His heart was as stoutly set on a seafaring career as it had been that March dawn when he crawled from his bedroom window and climbed down the ivy trunk to run away. He had been undeniably homesick, but that, he told himself, was because of the barbarous filth and cruelty of his surroundings.

It was home he was thinking of now, as he lay in the bight of the cable. Home, in the wooded, green Rhode Island valleys. It must be Summer now. He had lost track of dates, but he knew it was at least the middle of June. His father, solid New Englander, would be busy about the mill, his beard powdered white with the fragrant dust of the grain. He could see the wide mill-pond where the river spread placidly under overhanging elms. He could hear the rush of the water through the flume, the drip of the big mill-wheel, the steady rumble of the grinding stones. In the yard the farmers' horses would be lined up along the rail. In the kitchen, his mother, supervising old Martha at her cooking. And such cooking! He sighed a little at the memory of those light biscuits—those juicy pies.

Suddenly Jim was startled out of his musing by a heavy splash alongside the schooner. The sound was followed almost at once by a second and a third. The point from which the splashes came was hidden from him by the curve of the bow, but he could see the ripples spread and the quick gathering of sharks from far and near to the ship's side. In a moment there was a thrashing of tails as the brutes fought over their meal. It was the daily burial of the slaver's dead.

Jim heaved himself up to the deck once more. Time he got back to his quarters, for he knew the negroes would be brought up for an airing in a few moments. Sure enough, as he passed the main hatch, amidships, two of the sailors were lifting the heavy grating. There was an excited babble of sound from below, and Jarvis and the bo's'n, carrying cat-o'-nine-tails, went down through the opening. Facing the hatch towered Creadon, with a long black whip coiled in his hands, and the crew, variously armed with rope's ends and marline-spikes, waited about the deck.

Then two woolly heads appeared and two black bodies swung themselves up. A second couple followed and others behind them, each pair fettered ankle to ankle with an iron chain. As the slaves continued to pour up from the hatchway and crowd the deck, one thing was noticeable about all of them. Not one could stand erect when he first emerged. They stood pathetically bent and trembling, their muscles cramped from many hours in the hold, their bloodshot eyes blinking in the unaccustomed light.

At last nearly two hundred negroes had been herded on to the deck. Creadon shook out the long lash of his bull-whip. "All right," he roared—"now dance!"

Slowly, with a clanking of irons, the blacks began to lift their feet. Then, as the snaky length of the whip flicked in and out about their knees they moved faster, settling into a heavy rhythm that shook the ship from deck-beams to keelson. Here and there a slave too weak to raise his legs would tumble exhausted on the planks. These the bo's'n hauled out of the ranks and propped along the bulwarks. If a negro seemed particularly feeble, the surgeon was called to look him over. A few, suspected of shamming, were beaten with the cat until they got to their feet and resumed the awkward prancing.

This lasted for twenty minutes. At the end of that time the blacks were allowed to stand and breathe for a while. The mate moved among them, looking over their condition, poking them in the ribs or forcing open their mouths like a cattle drover. Once a negro held out his hands and begged for water as Creadon passed. He was answered with an oath and a blow on the jaw that felled him to the deck.

At the sight a lump of impotent anger swelled in Jim's throat. He turned away and went down to the cuddy. Sitting there dejected on the edge of his bunk, he tried to shut out the sounds from the deck—the steady tramp and clank as the negroes were marched to and fro, the crack of the whips, and the occasional barking of an order. It was approaching noon and the heat was intense. Jim knew how those blacks, sweltering in the sun, must be wanting water. Yet the second cupful of the day would not be given them till nightfall, when they were safely packed away in the slave-deck.

Suddenly the regular rhythm of the marching was broken. There was a confused scuffling noise above, and a high-pitched shout that swelled to the menacing howl of a hundred savage voices. The boy started to his feet and was met at the foot of the companion by the hurrying figure of the second mate. Jarvis was pale and breathless.

"Captain!" he cried, gasping. "Captain Hack! It's mutiny! The niggers are loose!" And he rushed to the big arms-chest in the corner of the cabin.

VIII

HE captain had been dozing in his chair by the table, the ever-present rum bottle at his elbow. He jumped to his feet when Jarvis yelled, and reached the arms-locker almost as soon as his second mate. In a few seconds they had laid out a tableful of pistols and muskets and were priming them. Then, thrusting two pistols into his belt and seizing a heavy cutlass, Hack made for the companionway.

"Load the rest, boy, and bring 'em on deck," he growled at Jim, over his shoulder.

Jarvis, similarly armed, followed him up the stairs, and a moment later Jim, clutching three muskets and another cutlass, went up after them.

The deck, from mainmast to fo'c'sle, was a seething, yelling turmoil. After the slaves' first rush, the sailors had rallied and beaten most of them back, away from the after deck. But one knot of struggling figures remained beside the water-butt—original objective of the negroes' charge. Creadon was down, and kneeling half across his body, striking him with huge bare fists, crouched the giant black chief. At the other end of the fetter that bound his ankle lay another negro, dead.

All this Jim took in at a single hurried glance. Then, as the sailors came to seize the muskets, he saw the captain's arm go up and heard the bitter *swish* of his cutlass blade. The big negro slumped backward, and Creadon crawled groggily to his feet.

The sight of the guns seemed to take the fight out of the blacks. Cowed and whimpering, they were whipped back, two by two, through the hatches, and went to their places in the reeking dark below with sullen, hopeless submission.

Four had been killed in the fight, and their bodies were heaved overboard without ceremony. The big African chief would have been disposed of in like manner except that he regained consciousness at the moment they laid hold of him. He had two ugly wounds where the captain's hanger had glanced off his head and buried itself in his shoulder. But he was too valuable to kill out of hand.

"Here, Dr. Brown," ordered Hack. "When you've done with the crew, patch this beggar up and see if he'll live."

THEY SHACKLED THE GIANT TO THE FOREMAST

They shackled the giant to the foremast in double chains and left him.

It was mid-afternoon before the deck had been cleaned and traces of the conflict removed. Then, in spite of misgivings on the part of the mates, Captain Hack gave orders to bring the women up for their daily exercise.

The noise of the *mêlée* above had reached them in their quarters in the after hold, and their excitement and terror were pitiful to see. No fetters bound the women or the children, but they clung together, panic-stricken, as they were driven on deck. Just as all had been assembled and they were beginning to grow quieter, there was a commotion in the middle of the group. A comely young negress with a year-old baby at her breast struggled out through the crowd. Her eyes were distraught as she turned searchingly from one white man to another. Holding the child out at arm's length, she knelt in front of the massive Creadon and sobbed out a few words in broken English that Jim recognized as a plea for water.

The baby's face was strangely wizened, and its tongue showed, thick and swollen.

"Get back there, you!" roared the mate. His whiplash cut the woman's naked side and she fell, writhing. As she lay there on the planks, clasping the infant to her, a deep-pitched groan of agony came from forward. There crouched the chief by the foremast, bending his mighty muscles in an effort to burst the chains that held him. Sweat rolled down his breast and arms. And if ever Jim saw murder in a face it was in the big black's as he glared at Creadon. As plainly as if the fact had been spoken, it was the torture of *his* woman—*his* baby—that the negro was watching.

Some of the other slaves lifted the girl to her feet and she cowered among them, her horror-stricken eyes fixed on her husband. It took a few minutes to restore order among the women, but at length, by the use of the cat, they were forced through the same drill that had been given the men. Jim looked on at the grim dance, his face pale and set with the resolve that was forming in his mind. He had heard the order given the night before and knew that no more water was to be allowed these poor wretches until the following morning. To the young wife of the chief and her baby it might mean the difference between life and death. Jim watched them closely when finally they were sent below decks once more. He contrived to slip into the slave deck behind the bo's'n and watched the stowing of the live cargo. There was scarcely room to sit erect in the shallow 'tween-decks.

The place occupied by the chief's woman and her child was right against the mainmast foot, not more than three yards from the bolted trap-door that Jim knew opened into the passage alongside his cuddy. He made careful note of the location, then turned silently and regained the deck before he was seen.

For what he planned to do he must wait until dusk should somewhat hide his movements. And yet he wanted to get it done before the ship's officers came below for their evening meal. The boy went into the cabin and looked about for something to occupy him in the interval. One job that needed doing was cleaning the glass in the ports. He got a bucket and rope and leaned out the square window in the stern, preparing to draw up water for the washing. There, just below him, he saw the ship's dinghy bobbing, and in it the carpenter, at work on the damaged rudder.

The man looked up and saw him. "Make fast that rope o' yours, lad," he said. "I'm comin' up. This job'll have to go over till mornin'."

Jim knotted the hempen line to a beam and peered out again. The carpenter passed up his hammer and saw, then tugged at the little boat's painter to make sure it was well tied.

"There," he said, at length, "now give me the bucket." When he had handed the water up to Jim he came swarming up himself and pulled the rope in after him. As the man went whistling forward, Jim stood for a long moment staring at the dinghy. Then, still thoughtful, he went about his window-cleaning.

After a while the color of the sea outside changed to a purple gray and the sky began to darken. Quietly the boy put away his bucket and went to a shelf of the cuddy. There was an old leather bottle with a strap and a stopper that he had often seen lying there. This he stuffed inside the roomy open front of his shirt, and went up the companionway, listening as he climbed. Voices came from aft by the wheel, and he could see some of the crew gathered forward. There was no one near the mainmast.

Moving in an aimless stroll, Jim went first to the rail and spat overboard as if he had nothing better to do. Then he walked slowly over to the water-butt. He pulled the mouth of the bottle out of his shirt and held it under the spigot, bending low as if he were drinking.

"Avast there, boy!" came a shout from the bo's'n forward. "Don't ye know the water's runnin' short?"

Jim shut off the spigot and stood erect with a guilty start. The canteen had slipped back inside his bosom, and he plugged in the stopper with one hand. Meanwhile he had presence of mind enough to wipe his mouth with the other.

Neither the afterguard nor the crew appeared to take any further notice of him. Still moving at a leisurely pace, he gained the companionway and descended, his heart pounding with excitement. At the end of the passage was the trap-door. He worked over the rusty bolt for a moment before it would slide. When at last it gave, he lifted the heavy trap, let himself down, and lowered the door after him again. Crouching there in the dark, he could feel the startled stir of bodies around him. The stench of foul air smote him like a blow. He waited, fearing an outcry, but none came. Three paces to the left! He moved slowly, gingerly, feeling for a space to put down his feet. Then his fumbling hand touched the broad curve of the mast and he knew he had reached his destination. Afraid of frightening the woman, he waited a moment till he heard her slow sobbing close below him.

"Sh-h!" he breathed, and touched her shoulder. Then he placed the canteen in her trembling hand. The negress took a bare taste of the water herself, then put the bottle to the baby's mouth. Jim could hear the child gurgle and choke over it. At last, still in silence, he felt the canteen pressed into his hand once more.

With infinite pains he retraced the few feet to the trap. Just as he reached it, a heavy step went past above. Captain Hack had come below. Jim waited till he was sure the captain was inside the cabin, then pushed upward cautiously and lifted the door, standing erect in the opening. All would have been well had not one of the black women caught sight of him then for the first time and given a scream of terror. The boy jerked himself up swiftly and was in the act of closing the trapdoor when of a sudden he saw Jethro Hack standing over him.

The captain's weather-lined face was dark with rage, but he said nothing, nor did he move. Only his blazing eyes followed Jim's as the boy rose and stood erect. Seconds passed slowly, and then the explosion came. Hack's big hand shot out and wrenched the canteen out of Jim's grasp.

"Yah, ye chicken-hearted thief!" he roared. "Sneakin' down here to stir up the niggers, eh? Takin' our water when every drop's needed! Let me tell one word o' this to the crew, an' they'll rip the livin' hide off ye. Time for that later. Tonight ye'll wait on us at table—after I'm done with ye!"

As he jerked out this speech, the captain seized Jim's wrist and pulled the boy after him into the cabin. Jim Slater was no coward, but his cheeks went white as he saw Hack reach up to the hook on the bulkhead where his favorite cat-o'-nine-tails hung. For a second the boy had a mad impulse to grapple with him and fight it out regardless of the consequences. Yet he knew his chances of escape would be slim indeed, even if he succeeded in besting the rugged shipmaster.

At that moment a heavy step came down the companion and Creadon entered. Hack ignored the mate. "Turn around," he ordered, and Jim turned, gripping the table edge with his hands.

Once, twice, three times—and steadily on till Jim's dizzy senses lost count—fell the cat. The knotted tongues of hide cut cruelly through his cotton shirt, welting his back and sides like white-hot iron bars. There was a rushing sound in his ears, and a blackness came and went before his eyes, but still he hung on stubbornly and refused to drop. At last, dimly, as if from a great distance, he heard the captain's panting voice.

"There, boy," it grated. "Go for'ard an' fetch the supper."

Reeling like a drunken man, Jim groped his way along

HE PLACED THE CANTEEN IN HER TREMBLING
HAND

the bulkhead, out of the cabin, up the companionway. The cooling breeze of evening came lightly across the shadowed deck. It roused his numbed brain and soothed the ache of his body. Standing there by the rail for a moment, he picked up enough strength to take him to the galley. The Portuguese looked intently at his drawn face but said nothing. Jim took the food for the cabin and made his way back.

The other members of the afterguard were at table when he entered. He went about serving, concentrating all his force of will on the immediate task. It was perhaps the best thing he could have done. Keeping constantly in motion prevented his bruises from stiffening. By the time the meal was over he was himself again. An occasional twinge from the welts under his blood-soaked shirt was the only effect remaining from his beating. He felt ready for whatever should come next. And in his own mind he had settled that.

Oftener even than usual, Jim poured fresh rum into the tankards on the table. The captain was drinking steadily, in the morose silence that was his habit after his temper had been loosed. The others kept up a desultory conversation for a while; then they too stopped talking.

At length the surgeon toppled forward over the table, dead drunk, and Creadon went swaying off to his berth. Jarvis remained sober enough to take his watch on deck. After he had left, Captain Hack still sat drinking, with no company but the snoring doctor and the watchful cabin-boy. After what seemed hours to Jim the captain rose. With fixed, unseeing eyes, he walked across the cabin, collided with the wall, and fell heavily. Jim waited long enough to hear his stertorous breathing mingle with the surgeon's, then tiptoed out.

Beside the cuddy in the passage lay the canteen, where the captain had hurled it. He picked it up, slipped his jack-knife into a trousers pocket, and went on deck.

There was little trouble about filling the leather bottle this time. Only the helmsman and the second mate were in sight. Jim slipped the strap over his shoulder and hid the canteen in his shirt as before. Then he walked quietly forward to the galley. The door was ajar, and looking in, he could see that the place was empty. Without a sound he slid through the door and went to the tall canisters where he knew the hard-tack was kept. Reaching in, he took half a dozen of the biscuits in his hand and was closing the lid when he heard a faint sound behind him. He whirled and saw, framed in the open door, the bearded silhouette of the cook.

IX

OR breathless seconds Jim stood frozen in his tracks. The burly Portuguese was likewise motionless, and Jim even began to hope that he had not been seen. Then the cook raised a hand in a warning gesture and moved silently inside the galley. When he was at the boy's side he turned his head as if listening. "*Sh-h-h!*" he whispered. He leaned so close to Jim that his beard brushed the lad's face. "W'at-a you do?" he asked. "You-a ron away?"

Jim made no answer. He saw the right hand of the Portuguese coming around from behind his back, where it had been hidden. A vision of the huge knife flashed across the boy's mind and he started back involuntarily. To his astonishment, the cook held a small package of some sort, which he pressed into Jim's hand.

" 'Ere," he whispered. "You tak-a! Bull-a-beef. You go'n-a be hongry."

As Jim gasped his thanks, the man turned and vanished as quietly as he had appeared. The beef was rolled
up in a square of waterproof tarpaulin. Jim opened it,
put in his ship's-biscuit, and wrapped it tightly once
more, stowing it for safekeeping in the back of his shirt.
Then he stole out of the galley and looked warily up and
down the length of the schooner. The two quiet figures
still stood aft by the wheel. Three or four of the crew
were swapping yarns in the shadow to starboard of the
fo'c's'le, and the fettered Congo chief lay quiet by the
mast. Otherwise the deck was deserted.

Jim drew a long breath. It was now or never. Silently
as a ghost he moved forward, passed the fo'c's'le on the
port side, and picked his way between coils of rope to
the peak of the bow. As he eased his body down into the
loop of the cable, a long streak of phosphorescence cut
the oily blackness under the bow. Jim shuddered, recall-
ing the ever-vigilant convoy of sharks that had surrounded the ship that morning. Even now he knew they
were waiting somewhere out there in the circle of the
dark. If he dropped with a splash they would be on him
like a pack of wolves.

Only a moment he hesitated, steeling his nerves, planning what he had to do. Then he turned, facing the side
and let himself down, inch by inch, into the cool Gulf
water. It rose to his waist, to his breast, and he was hanging at arm's length. Nothing for it now but to drop. He
kept both arms extended over his head and let go, slip-

ping straight downward with scarcely a ripple. His head went under, then bobbed up again. With slow caution he began to work his way aft along the bulge of the bows. Yard after yard he made, feeling the rough barnacles of the hull beneath his hands.

He was past the ship's waist now, and drawing close to his goal. Then through the sound of the blood pounding in his ears, he caught another sound—a rippling rush in the water behind him. As he turned his head an enormous whitish shape loomed in the sea just under the surface. It was a monster shark. Jim saw it roll sidewise and caught the gleam of teeth, edging the vague black triangle of its mouth. For an instant he was paralyzed with fright, and his very stillness saved him. The brute steered off, barely brushing him with a fin as it passed.

The boy could see the side of the dinghy, now only five or six yards away. The shark was swinging out in a wide circle, possibly preparing for another rush. Jim could not stay where he was. In a flash he decided to swim for it. He gave himself a push along the side and cut aft with strong, quick strokes. His outstretched hand felt the planking of the boat—reached upward to the gunwale. With a final gasping effort the boy hauled himself over and tumbled into the dinghy. And inches from his leg, as he left the water, the shark's teeth came together with an empty snap.

For long minutes Jim lay quiet in the bottom of the boat. He did not think he could be seen from the deck in the darkness. And if any sound of his flight had been heard aboard, there surely would be a commotion by this time. At last he dared raise his head and hitch forward across the center thwart till he could reach the painter at the bow. His wet fingers fumbled ineffectually at the knot and finally he pulled out his jack-knife and cut the rope, close to the ship.

With the maddening slowness of a moving clock-hand the space between the little craft and the big one widened. Jim sat motionless and watched the stretch of shadowy water till his muscles ached with the tension. There was a pair of oars in the boat, but he feared to use them because he knew the thole-pins would make a noise. A little breeze came past his face. He looked up at the sagging sails of the schooner and saw the main boom swing outward slowly to an accompanying creak of blocks. Almost imperceptibly at first, the ship gathered way. An order to the helmsman came faintly back to the drifting dinghy. And Jim breathed a deep sigh of relief, for he knew he had accomplished the first step in his escape.

Still doubtful about the noise that might arise if he tried to row, the boy took a single oar and seated himself on the stern thwart of the little boat. He used the oar like a canoe paddle, dipping it alongside. At first Jim's only thought was to put distance between himself and the hated *White Angel*. He paddled straight into the wind because the schooner was moving in the opposite direction. But soon he realized that the dinghy could no longer be seen from the ship's deck and that it was time he headed for shore if he ever hoped to get there. The night was moonless but fairly clear. Jim located the Dipper and followed the line of the "pointers" upward to the North Star. As he recalled it, the land they had sighted that morning had lain a point or two west of north. He placed both oars in the tholes and swung the bow of his bobbing little craft till it headed northward. Astern he sighted a group of stars by which to steer, spat on his hands, and started to row.

For what must have been nearly an hour Jim pulled steadily. Then, his muscles aching with the unwonted labor, he turned hopefully to see if the shore was yet in sight. Only the immensity of the Gulf, ruffled by a fitful night wind, stretched to the dark horizon. It was as if he had spent his energy in standing still. Yet he told himself he surely must have made some headway. A moment only he rested and then set manfully to work again.

That was the longest night Jim Slater had ever spent. Hour after hour of back-breaking labor that seemed to get him nowhere. The stars wheeled up across the sky, and he had repeatedly to pick new bearings in order to keep on his course. He shuddered when he thought what might have been his fate if there had been clouds to hide the heavens.

The time came when Jim's overtired arms could no longer move the oars. Drugged with weariness, he had barely strength enough left to pull the blades inboard before he slumped down in the bottom of the boat. That was the last thing he remembered.

When he woke it was daylight and the dinghy was dancing to the chop of the morning breeze. Struggling upward out of the sleep of exhaustion, he looked blankly about him at the blue waves for a moment before he recalled where he was. A terrible stiffness cramped his back and arms and his throat was dry with thirst. He reached for the leather canteen and drank from it greedily. Then he munched a piece of hard-tack and began to feel better.

The wind, he realized, might have drifted the dinghy far, while he slept. Which way? he wondered, in sudden panic. And then, looking over the blunt bow of the little boat, he saw a sight that made his heart bound. There, scarcely a league distant, was a low, green, tree-clad shore!

Before he started to row once more, Jim stood erect and shaded his eyes as he searched the sea astern. After long staring he finally made out a tiny gray speck—a vessel, hull down on the horizon to the southward. Whether it was the *White Angel* he could not tell, but in any case it was too far off to bother him now.

With renewed energy he picked up his oars and pulled for the land. The sun shone fiercely into the boat, and Jim's hands were bleeding from a dozen broken blisters, but he stuck to his rowing. Now and then he turned exultantly to see the shoreline drawing close. At last he found himself entering a broad channel between sand-bars. Beyond lay a lagoon, dotted with more bars and reedy islets, and then the sandy beach rising into a dark green jungle.

There was no sign of a town or a human habitation, but the wild life of the coast swarmed everywhere around him. Herons stalked in the edge of the reeds and heavy-bodied pelicans flapped past, intent on their fishing. Snow-white gulls filled the air with cries as they sailed and dipped above the water. On a low spit of sand he saw a huge turtle move slowly in the sun.

Jim leaned on his oars and looked to east and west along the shore. To all appearances he might have been the only human being left alive, and for a moment his loneliness frightened him. Brought up as he had been, on the thickly settled seaboard of New England, the idea that he might be landing on a vast stretch of uninhabited coast had simply never occurred to him.

Where was he, he wondered, and in which direction did civilization lie? Then he laughed at his own fears. He was free at last. He was done with the slave-ship and all he had endured aboard her. He was strong—ready for any adventure. For the present at least he realized his problem was to find food and fresh water. Not even shelter was necessary as long as the weather stayed clear.

Paddling leisurely, Jim crossed the lagoon and ran the bow of the dinghy up into the sand. Above were tangled trees, hung with long gray streamers of Spanish moss. In and out of their shadowy coolness darted small bright-

plumaged birds, and great blue butterflies floated lazily
among the branches. In that inviting shade, thought
Jim, he would surely find water. He crawled stiffly out
of the boat and climbed the sand. But at the edge of the
jungle he stopped in consternation. The matted snarl of
vegetation reached from the ground high into the trees,
as thick and impenetrable as a wall. Twice he attacked
it with knife and hands, burrowing resolutely into the
green mass, only to find his way hopelessly blocked at the
end of a few yards. Puzzled, he walked along the beach
for nearly a mile, hoping to find a rill flowing down from
some spring. When he got back to the boat he was hot
and thirsty. Under the stern thwart lay his leather bottle,
and he looked at it longingly, lifted it, shook it. From
the weight and sound he judged that the canteen was
about half full. A pint of water or less, to last him he
could not tell how long. No, he decided, he didn't need
a drink just then.

Jim shoved off and started to row once more, cruising
westward along the beach. As he scanned the shore for
some sign of a stream emptying into the sea, he caught
sight of another turtle, waddling down the sand. Perhaps
he might catch one and kill it for food. On the impulse
of the moment he turned the boat inshore and approached
the spot where the turtle had taken to the water. Looking
over the side, he had a single glimpse of the big beast,
swimming leisurely away through the green depths. The

only way to capture one, he decided, would be to surprise it on land.

Just as he was swinging the dinghy's bow outward again there was a flutter of long wings and a big white gull settled down on the beach, close above the place where he had noticed the turtle. Paying no attention to him, the bird balanced itself awkwardly and started scratching with its clumsy little feet in the sand. It uncovered something after a moment's work. Jim saw it lift a rounded brownish object in its beak and go winging off toward the sand-bars.

Turtle's eggs! He had heard Johnny Buck, the old wrecker on the slave-ship, tell of finding them along the Florida Keys. No sooner had he grounded the boat than he ran up the beach to the shallow depression that the gull had visited. Where the sand was partly scratched away he dug with his hands and soon unearthed more than a dozen of the leathery globes, left there by the female turtle for the sun to hatch.

Jim had no flint and steel nor any other means of building a fire. However, he was too hungry to be particular. With the point of his knife he made an opening in one of the eggs and he sucked the raw contents. Contrary to his expectations, there was no unpleasant or fishy taste. It was palatable enough to make him want another. When he had satisfied the first craving for food he put the rest of the eggs with his canteen and hard-tack, under the thwart. Then he set out once more.

The boy paddled along the shore all the morning and through most of the afternoon, until his blistered hands started to bleed again. The fresh-water creek he had hoped to discover was still missing. At last he carefully measured half of his remaining water and drank slowly, holding it in his mouth as long as he could.

As he had proceeded, the coast had grown more and more irregular. He hauled out on a curving stretch of beach and lay down to rest on the sand, a little way above the boat.

Hours later Jim was roused suddenly out of a heavy sleep. It was the cold touch of water on his bare feet that had wakened him. Sitting up with a start, he realized that the tide had risen and the boat was gone. At first he could not see it, in the dusk of the early evening, and panic seized him. Then, looking frantically up and down the beach, he sighted the little craft rocking on the waves, a quarter of a mile further along the shore.

The tide, still rising, had prevented the dinghy from drifting far from land, and when Jim came abreast of it he found the boat was not more than fifty yards out. Quickly he stripped off the tattered shirt and duck trousers that had been his only clothing when he left the schooner, and dropped them in a heap on the beach.

The low waves, breaking against his legs, felt cold as he waded in. A surprisingly strong current was setting along the shore to the westward. He shivered and stumbled forward till the water reached his breast, then started to swim strongly in the direction of the boat. Soon he realized that it would be a long pull, for the dinghy was moving almost as fast as he was. The exercise had warmed him now and he settled down to a steady stroke that brought him gradually nearer to the drifting craft.

After twenty minutes of hard swimming Jim finally reached the boat's side. He took a moment's rest, holding on to the gunwale, and pulled himself aboard. The row to the beach was soon accomplished, but when he hauled out on the sand night had fallen. He pulled the craft far enough above the tide line to assure its staying where he left it and turned back to get his clothes.

The drift, he realized, must have carried him some distance. Picking his way along the beach in the dark, he kept watch to right and left and presently felt sure he had reached the place where he had undressed. There were patches of weed and bits of driftwood on the sand that looked familiar in the gloom, and yet he found no trace of his garments.

Jim began to be worried. His jack-knife was his sole weapon, and that he had left in his trousers pocket. The clothes, too—light as they were—had served as protection from the sun and from the evening chill. He hunted up and down the beach for the best part of an hour without result. At last it seemed the wisest thing he could do was to return to the boat and search again in daylight.

He trotted back up the shore and saw the dark shape

of the dinghy looming ahead of him. He would turn it over, he decided, and sleep in its shelter.

Then, just as he took hold of the boat's side, he heard a sound. It came faint and distant but unmistakable through the stillness of the night—a peal of boisterous laughter.

X

HE utter unexpectedness of that sound of human voices on the desolate beach made Jim's heart jump into his mouth. It had come, he was certain, from somewhere up the shore to the west. Staring in that direction, he saw a dim red glow above the trees—a fire. His first impulse was to run toward it, but a chill of fear made him pause. Could it have been made by the crew of the slaver, landing to discharge their smuggled cargo? There was only one thing to do, and that was to find out without being seen.

Naked as he was, the boy went cautiously along the sand, watching the red in the sky deepen as he drew closer. At first it seemed to him that the fire was somewhere back in the woods. Then he realized that he was moving along a narrow point, for he could catch the gleam of water from the other side of the trees. He went on till he could plainly hear men's voices and see the flicker of flames through the tangled undergrowth.

Jim dropped to his hands and knees and crawled forward into the brush. The vines and creepers made his movements slow, but he pushed on an inch at a time and soon found that by rising erect on his knees he could command a full view of the fire.

It was a roaring blaze of driftwood logs, midway down a beach of sand that pitched steeply into the lagoon. Beyond it, ruddy in the firelight, rose the masts and rigging of a small black schooner. She was moored within a dozen yards of land, and from her deck to the shore a long plank had been laid. Up this plank, as Jim watched, a barefooted seaman was rolling a cask. And clustered about the fire, a score of others were singing and shouting. A curious thrill went through Jim as he watched them. He had never set eyes on a pirate, but he had seen pictures and heard tales of the sea-rovers ever since he could remember. And if ever men bore the distinguishing marks of the pirate breed these did.

They were of all nationalities, seemingly—French and Spanish Creoles of the Gulf, swarthy Portuguese, and here and there a big-boned renegade of Yankee or British stock. They wore broad, vivid sashes, and huge earrings gleamed below their bright bandannas. Jim had never seen such a display of pistols and sheath-knives. And they had faces as hard and cruel as their steel. All, that is, except the captain. He was a huge, burly-shouldered man with merry eyes and a blond beard through which

IF EVER MEN BORE THE DISTINGUISHING MARKS
OF THE PIRATE BREED THESE DID

his teeth shone white when he laughed. Jim picked him as the leader of the group because of his easy air of authority as he stood beside the fire. The orders he gave were in some foreign tongue—French, the boy thought. But when he spoke, the men addressed jumped quickly to obey.

There were half a dozen of them at work, trundling empty water-casks along the beach from the schooner and filling them at a spring among the trees. Fresh water! Jim was gladdened mightily by the sight. Once the pirates had finished their watering, he promised himself a long, cool drink.

At last it appeared that no more casks were to be filled. One by one the pirates ended their labor and joined the group around the bonfire. A keg of rum had been produced from somewhere aboard the vessel. Every man filled his tin cup at the bung and swung into the howling chorus of a Creole chantey. Jim watched them prancing and singing, fascinated by the wild rhythm. But when the song was at its height, his eye was suddenly caught by a stealthy movement on the schooner's deck. He was sure he had seen a man ducking along behind the bulwark, making for the after part of the ship.

The figure went out of sight for a moment, then reappeared at the rail. The pirates were too preoccupied with their revelry to notice what was happening, but Jim, from his hiding-place, could watch every motion the man made. He was not very tall, and his face, in the dim glow of the fire, looked young and scared. In one hand he carried a musket, shot-pouch, and powder-flask. In the crook of his other arm was a long-haired little dog. At the top of the gangplank he seemed to hesitate, glancing back and forth along the bank.

The shore end of the long board was a little to the right of the bonfire, in the same direction as the spring. With catlike caution the man moved down the plank, watching the group at the fire as he came. When he reached the foot he turned like a frightened animal and started to run down the shore.

Almost at the same moment the carousing pirates caught sight of him. There was a yell in Creole French—*"Regardez! Il se sauve!"* And a dozen buccaneers leaped after the flying figure.

Leading by twenty paces and running with the speed of fear, the man neared the cover of the woods. Jim's sympathy was all with the fugitive, and he rose to his knees in the excitement of the moment, urging him on with whispered words. Then, just as it seemed he would escape, there was a hurtling flash of steel and a cry that chilled Jim's blood. One of the foremost pirates had flung his knife with unerring aim at the back of the flee-ing man. Strangely, the victim did not fall. Still holding to his gun, he dove after the dog into the thick growth of reeds and bushes beyond the spring. Jim had a sickening impression of the bent back and the hilt of the knife showing horribly between the shoulder blades. Then the undergrowth closed with a swish.

Some of the pirates would have followed headlong, but a warning shout made them pause. "Look out! He'll shoot!" some one cried. And then another voice—"He's done for. Let him die. That was a beauty, Pedro—right to the spot!"

There was a growl of disappointment from one or two of the men, but most of them were quick to back away from the ominously quiet thicket where their victim had disappeared. One by one they returned to the fire, but the pleasure seemed to have gone out of their merry-making. They talked in low tones and kept one eye on the dark wall of the woods.

The big pirate chief was standing on the side of the blaze nearest Jim, and the boy could overhear a part of the conversation between him and one of his lieutenants —a cockney sailor with a twisted shoulder and a mean, unshaven face.

"'Ere, skipper," the pirate was saying, "this plice don't feel so 'ealthy to me. If 'e ain't dead, that beggar could tike a pot-shot right into us, a-standin' 'ere. Besides—that cutter we sighted—" His voice dropped too low for Jim's ear, but the boy could see the captain nod in agreement.

"*Tenez donc!*" shouted the pirate leader. "*A bord! Vite!*" And the crew obeyed with alacrity, picking up their cannikins and mounting the plank to the deck. The captain and his cockney counselor stopped long enough to kick some sand on the embers of the fire, then followed them aboard.

Jim kept to his hiding-place. He watched the buccaneers pole their schooner off into deeper water and run up the sails. Then, as her canvas caught the light night breeze, the black-hulled vessel moved slowly out into the cove. Jim was chilled and stiff when at last he unbent his cramped muscles. A dull glow still came from the ashes of the pirate fire, and he crouched beside it, turning first one side of his naked body and then the other to the grateful warmth.

When he felt sure that the schooner was out of sight around the point, Jim brought some dry sticks and rekindled the dying embers. He had no wish to attract the attention of the pirates; so he kept the blaze small, laying his wood in a cone-shaped heap like an Indian's cooking-fire. At least it would warm him, and if he kept it burning till morning he could cook some of his turtle eggs.

Now, for the first time in hours, he realized how thirsty he was. Working his way back through the ridge of trees, he ran down to the dinghy, found his canteen, and returned with it to the shore of the inner lagoon. On the way he picked up a dry branch to use for a torch. He held one end of it in the fire till it was blazing brightly and then set out along the beach toward the spring.

Somewhere in the woods a night bird cried. In the eery

stillness that followed, Jim could hear no sound but the pad of his own feet and the crackle of the burning stick in his hand. He traced the pirates' foot-prints down the beach to the place where he had seen them roll their casks. There he found a little stream of water running down through a narrow channel into the lagoon. And at the source, bowered in green leaves, was a circular basin with fresh, clear water bubbling out of the white sand that formed its bottom.

Jim knelt eagerly on the moss at the spring's edge and plunged his face into that refreshing coolness. He drank long and deep. Then, just as he was dipping the leather bottle into the water, he heard something that brought him suddenly to his feet. It was a low groan, and it seemed to come from the undergrowth off to the left.

He waited, scarcely breathing. The sound was not re-peated, but a moment later came the soft, troubled whine of a dog. Jim thought quickly. The wounded pirate was still alive. He must go into the brush and find him—do something for him if he could. If he took a light he might be mistaken for an enemy and fired on. The torch had ceased to flame, but it had a live ember at its tip. He picked it up, together with the full canteen, and started into the thicket.

With nothing to guide him save a vague memory of the direction from which the sounds had come, Jim groped his way forward, foot by foot. At last he paused, afraid of stepping on the man in the darkness.

"Hallo!" he called softly, and instantly a frenzy of barking broke out right ahead of him. Jim took a step forward and spoke again, through chattering teeth. "It's all right," he said. "They've all gone. I'm a friend. I want to help you."

The dog had ceased barking and there was a long moment of silence. Then a weak voice answered in broken English: "Come closer. Let me see you."

The boy blew on the live spark at the tip of his torch and nursed it into flame. Holding the burning stick above his head, he took another stride forward and found himself looking down through interlacing vines at a still, white figure on the ground. At the same moment the little dog charged valiantly at his legs.

"*A moi, Dodo!*" gasped the wounded man, and the animal, a brown water spaniel, rushed back to his side.

Jim knelt and gently lifted the man's head. "Here's some water," he said. "Can you drink it?"

The other nodded eagerly. But as the liquid poured down his throat a stricken look came into his eyes and he choked horribly.

"The knife," he breathed at last. "It is in my lung. I am dying."

Jim eased him down once more on his side and waited, helplessly.

"Who are you?" asked the wounded man after a moment.

"Jim Slater, of Rhode Island," the boy replied. "I ran

away from a Yankee slaver, and I'm trying to find a town or a settlement so I can get home."

"Ah," said the other wistfully. "Poor boy. But you will live. You will reach your home." He spoke with the accent of the Louisiana French. "I will tell you," he went on. "This is the shore of Mississippi Sound. To the west is New Orleans. Four days if you had a boat. Seven if you walk, as I hoped to walk. I, too, ran away." He paused, fighting for breath, then went on slowly. "I am Dieudonné LeGros"—he said it with a touch of pride— "son of the shipowner. I was supercargo of the barque *La Belle Rivière*. Two days outside the Balize we were attacked by pirates. It was 'Barbe Blonde' who led them —'Yellow Beard,' as the Americans call him. There was much killing, but me they kept alive. Two months I have been on their ship, waiting for this chance."

Again he lay quiet, mustering his ebbing strength. His voice, when he spoke again, was a bare whisper. "Soon," he said, "very soon, I will be gone. Take my little Dodo. Take my clothes—my gun. They will help you on your journey." There was a pause while he fumbled in the breast of his shirt. "Take this, too," he murmured, holding up something in his hand. "Take it to my mother— Madame LeGros, in the Petite Rue St. Jean."

He crossed himself and started to whisper the words of a Catholic prayer. But in the middle of it his lips ceased to move. Jim leaned close and laid his ear against the young Creole's breast. He was dead.

With a heavy heart Jim lifted the body under the armpits and dragged it out through the brush to the beach. There, by the light of his little fire, he slowly removed the blood-stained shirt, the loose seaman's trousers of striped blue and white drill, the shoes and socks. Then he scooped a long hole in the sand above the tide line and laid Dieudonné LeGros to rest. When the sand was replaced he took the wicked-looking seaman's dirk he had pulled from the wound and whittled two sticks for a cross. Binding the cross-bar to the upright stick with the green stem of a creeper, he thrust the rude marker into the sand at the grave's head.

All through this simple burial the little brown spaniel had lain close by, with his nose on his paws. When it was finished he went slowly to the grave, sniffed the sand, and lifted his head in a single long, plaintive howl—a requiem for his dead master.

Jim went over to the fire and bent close, to examine the token given him by the dying Frenchman. It was a small cameo of a charming woman's profile, bound with gold and suspended by a delicate gold chain. On the back were engraved the words, *"A mon fils, 1820."* It had been given him by his mother, thought Jim, only the year before.

There was a lump in his throat as he picked up the gun and the clothes.

"Come on, Dodo," he said gruffly, and led the way back to the dinghy on the outer beach.

XI

N THE shelter of the overturned boat Jim slumbered heavily till the sun on his face awoke him. Then he sat up, stretching his arms. Suddenly he saw the spaniel lying beside him, and the events of the past night came back to him with a rush. The little dog's eyes were full of sadness, but he wagged his tail slowly and got to his feet.

Jim looked at him and grinned. "Well, little fellow," he said, "it's you and me together—a couple of orphans. It's going to take something to feed you, but I guess I'm glad you're here." He held out his hand, and the spaniel caressed his fingers with an eager red tongue.

Jim found it pleasant to have something to talk to. "Anyhow, Dodo," he went on, "we've got a gun now, so we ought to be able to get us some birds." He picked up the musket and examined it. Firearms were no mystery to him. He found the gun clean and well cared for, with a fresh flint in the lock. The powder flask was filled to the brim and there were plenty of bullets in the pouch.

Jim pulled on the striped pirate trousers that LeGros had worn, and washed out the blood-stained shirt, spreading it on the dinghy's bottom in the sun. While it was drying he took the gun and walked down the beach for nearly half a mile, hoping to find his own clothes. The garments themselves had been so ragged that he did not mind their loss, but his pocket-knife was of real value to him. No trace of the clothing was to be found, and he concluded the tide had risen and swept it away.

When he returned, the shirt was dry enough to put on. The Creole's shoes, Jim found, were too small for his feet; so he left them on the beach. Righting the boat and hauling it to the water's edge was the work of a moment, and as soon as he had stowed the musket, ammunition, and canteen he was ready to resume his voyage.

"All right, Dodo," he ordered, "jump in. We'll look for something to eat as we go."

With the silky-haired spaniel sitting gravely in the stern, Jim pulled out from shore and started to move westward along the beach. He had been rowing only a few minutes when a pair of mallard ducks went by overhead. They were losing altitude as they neared the land and appeared to be headed for the inner cove, behind the point.

Jim swung the bow inshore and rowed hard. No sooner had he beached the boat than he was running up the sand, gun in hand. At the edge of the thicket he paused to load, then went on through the screening trees as quietly as possible. After a moment he had a clear view of the lagoon ahead, and sure enough, there were the ducks, swimming along at the edge of the reeds. The distance was not above forty yards. The boy knelt and took careful aim at the drake's bright-plumaged body. At the report of the musket both ducks fluttered, but to Jim's consternation the ball flew high and to the left, raising a spurt of white where it hit the water.

The birds did not take wing but started to swim rapidly. Dodo had stayed close to Jim's side, silent, quivering with excitement. Hurriedly reloading, the boy ran on a few steps, then settled himself for another shot. This time he deliberately aimed a little to the right of the nearer bird and close to the water line.

Bang! As the smoke lifted he saw the drake flap his wings and then tumble back into the water, while the female duck flew swiftly off. Dodo did not wait for a word of command. He was away like a flash, plunging into the lagoon and paddling out to the dead bird that floated a dozen yards from shore.

When the spaniel returned, proudly bearing the game in his mouth, Jim gave him an enthusiastic welcome. "You and I can work together, dog," he said, as he stroked the sleek brown head. "As long as I've found out how to hold this crooked gun, we ought to be able to make a go of it. Now, then, how about some breakfast?"

Jim rustled up an armful of driftwood and whittled a little heap of fine, dry shavings. Then he laid his fire carefully, and putting a pinch of gunpowder in the priming-pan of his musket, snapped the flint, close to the tinder. In no time at all he had a fine blaze going.

While the fire was forming a bed of coals Jim plucked and cleaned the dead duck. He had no salt, but he thought soaking the meat in salt water might help to season it. On the beach he found a mass of drifted sea-weed that had a salty taste, and stuffed his duck with a handful of the leathery brown pods. By the time he finished, there was a deep bed of live embers. Jim scooped a hollow in the sand, raked some of the coals into it, and laid the bird on top, wrapped in green leaves. Then he filled in around it with red ashes and covered the make-shift oven with leaves and sand.

"There, Dodo," he told the spaniel, "it'll take a while for that to cook, and we may as well do some exploring."

Gun in hand, he led the way along the shore of the cove to the place where the pirates had had their fire, then on, past the grave of LeGros, to the spring. When he and the dog had drunk their fill, he went back to the water's edge.

There were no more birds in sight, but down at the bottom of the lagoon among the roots of the reeds Jim could see good-sized crabs moving about. He rolled up his trousers and waded in, trying to catch one with his hands. Each time he approached, the agile crustaceans would scuttle off out of his reach, and he soon decided that some other method must be found.

For a moment he stood thinking, then called Dodo and started back through the woods to the outer beach. The Creole's shoes were still where he had left them, and he quickly pulled out the laces. Then another idea occurred to him. His wits were beginning to sharpen. Necessity was making him find new uses for things. He picked up the shoes and returned to the place where he had cleaned the duck. He had left the long pirate knife there because he had no easy way to carry it. Now he cut a broad strip of leather from one of the shoes and fashioned a half-sheath to hold the dirk. With another leather strap he bound the sheath to the side of his trousers through two holes slashed in the waist-band.

Next Jim looked around till he found a piece of fat, removed from the body of the drake. He knotted the two shoestrings together and tied the scrap of offal to one end. He had seen crabs caught in the Providence River and knew something about their tastes.

Wading a little way into the cove, he dangled his bait in the water and let it sink slowly toward the bottom. With a rush the crabs arrived. There was a rough-and-tumble battle for the piece of fat, but the biggest crab won. He seized the bait with both powerful claws, and a second later Jim had hauled him out on shore.

In almost less time than it takes to tell it, four more of the hungry beasts had been added to the larder. Jim had no way to boil them, lacking any sort of pot, but he had seen clams and oysters baked in seaweed and thought the same method might be used for crabs. For the present he put them in the dinghy, where he could keep them alive.

About noon both the boy and the dog had developed ravenous appetites. Jim lifted part of the cover of his beach oven and sniffed at the steam that emerged. It smelled so savory that he was sure the duck must be done, and digging in with a stick he soon unearthed the fowl.

There followed such a meal as the young Rhode Islander had not known in months. True, the mallard was somewhat tough and could have stood more cooking, but to his starved palate it tasted like a culinary triumph. Dodo, who gnawed the bones that Jim tossed him, seemed to find the repast equally satisfying. They ate till there was nothing left. Then Jim raced the dog back to the spring for a last drink before leaving the pirates' cove.

With a full canteen and a commissary increased by half a dozen lively crabs, they started their voyage in earnest. Jim's blisters had healed sufficiently so that it no longer hurt him to row. All through the hot afternoon he pulled up the sound, skirting islands and sandy points, with the dark green line of live oaks and magnolias always in sight to starboard.

Two or three times he saw the sails of fishing craft at a distance—small sloops and luggers with patched and dirty canvas. They paid no attention to him and he was never close enough to hail them, so he kept on his way.

Toward dusk Jim swung the bow of the dinghy inshore and pulled for the beach. The waves had risen with a freshening breeze, but he was able to run in without difficulty through the low surf.

When he had built a fire in the shelter of the boat, the boy dug a pit and collected some wet seaweed preparatory to cooking his crabs. He heated a couple of good-sized stones till they sizzled when water touched them. Then he tumbled them into the hole in the sand. Each crab was stunned by a blow on the head and wrapped in the wet weed. Next he piled them on top of the stones and covered the mass with a thick layer of sand, poking a hole in the top for steam to escape. While they were cooking he took Dodo and set out to reconnoiter.

Just beyond where Jim had landed, the shore curved northward toward the mouth of a broad estuary. On the other side of the stretch of water, two or three miles from where he stood, lights were twinkling in the gathering dark. This was no pirate fire, he was sure; there was no glow in the sky, and the lights burned steadily in a scattered cluster. He was near a settlement at last.

Jim was too tired to search for fresh water, so he divided the contents of the leather bottle with Dodo and fell to on the crabs. He found them juicy, tender, and well cooked, and three of them made a good supper for himself and the dog. The rest he placed in the bottom of the boat for future use. Then the two wanderers curled themselves up on the sand beside the fire and were soon asleep.

The spaniel's barking woke Jim just after dawn. He sat up, rubbing his eyes, and reached for the musket in alarm. However, it was not danger that had roused the dog. A flight of ducks was winging seaward, low overhead. The boy hastily primed his gun and took a quick shot as the last of the birds went past. By a lucky chance his ball reached its mark and one of the ducks fell into the surf, where Dodo raced to retrieve it.

Jim was exuberant. "That was shootin', dog!" he cried. "I guess ol' Dan'el Boone himself would have been satisfied with that one." He tossed the bird into the boat along with the rest of his meager belongings and made ready for a start. When the bow of the dinghy was in the surf Jim took his place behind it and waited till a wave broke. Then he ran the boat straight out through the next one and scrambled in over the stern in time to catch up the oars before his craft could swing sidewise into the trough.

The morning wind blew up from the south against an ebb tide running out of the estuary. It raised short, choppy seas through which the boat thrashed clumsily. For more than an hour Jim pulled at the oars, glancing over his shoulder now and then at the opposite point of land. It was well into the morning when he finally pulled clear of the tide-rip and approached a row of fishermen's shanties lifted on stilts above the beach. A long, rickety pier jutted out from shore, and moored along its sides were two disreputable-looking coasting schooners and a dozen smaller craft.

The boy ran his dinghy in past the vessels and beached it close to the crazy piling of the pier. Two dark-visaged, scantily-clad men were spreading a net to dry farther along the beach. They stared at him curiously while he hauled up the boat, but offered no sign of welcome. Jim stood undecided for a moment, then told Dodo to guard the dinghy, and took his way up a sandy cart-track leading to the street of the village.

A row of mean little houses with a dilapidated store or two made up the settlement. A big yellow hound lay dozing in the sun, twitching his ears to drive away the flies. Otherwise the street was deserted. Jim climbed the low stoop of the nearest store and looked in at the open door. The place was so dark that at first he could see little, but presently a man appeared from behind a dusty counter heaped with a jumble of goods. He shot a keen look at Jim, evidently taking in his blue eyes and freckled Yankee face, for he made no effort to address him in French.

"W'at you wan', eh?" the storekeeper asked.

"I'm trying to get to New Orleans," Jim replied. "And I wondered if I could get some water and maybe something to eat."

The man eyed him suspiciously a moment, then with a

scowl and a shrug he half turned away. Jim could see he had sized him up as having no money for trade.

"Water—yes," said the storekeeper, jerking his thumb in the direction of a wooden pump farther up the street. "Food—I don' know. Dose shrimpers hain' got much."

With that the man swung on his heel and went back inside the store. There was nothing for Jim to do but move on. He approached the door of the next house and rapped, but no one answered. Still undiscouraged, the boy went to the third shack in the row. Here the door stood open, and he heard voices inside. At his knock a fat, barefooted woman in a slatternly dress came and frowned at him. Politely he repeated his request for food. As if his words had released a spring, she flourished her arms in a sudden gesture and started to pour out a babble of French. Jim could understand only a word or two of what she said, but he gathered that his ancestors were pigs and that it would be better for him if he took himself off.

Flushing with anger, Jim bowed stiffly and strode back to the beach. He would get some water, he decided, and be on his way. As the boy was leaving the boat with the leather bottle in his hand, his eye chanced to light on a big calabash gourd lying on the sand. He went over and picked it up. A little salt water dribbled out when he tipped the neck. Whether it had fallen from the pier or been drifted up by the tide he could not tell, but he had no scruples about taking possession of it. With a reassuring word to Dodo he returned to the village street and filled both the canteen and the gourd at the pump.

It was just as he passed the shore end of the pier on his way back that Jim heard a disturbing sound. It came from the direction of his boat—the hoarse, gasping snarl of fighting dogs. The boy quickened his steps to a run and dashed down the cart-track to the beach. There stood Dodo beside the boat, teeth bared, valorously facing the gaunt yellow hound that Jim had seen in the road. The big dog charged in fiercely, bowling the spaniel over and gashing his shoulder with a chop of his long fangs. And then Jim came to the rescue. He was swinging a stick of driftwood snatched from the beach, and as the hound's teeth reached for Dodo's throat, the club caught him in the ribs and knocked him sidewise, yelping.

There was no more fight left in the dog, but now danger threatened from a different source. Jim, lifting Dodo into the dinghy, looked up to see the two fishermen running toward him along the beach. The nearest one was already within a dozen yards, and his face, contorted with anger, told Jim that he meant trouble. The boy flung the canteen and the calabash into the boat and heaved mightily under the bow. The craft slid halfway into the water, but before Jim could give it the final shove, his attacker was upon him.

"My dog—you keel 'eem!" the man yelled, and launched his big body at the boy. Jim had dropped the club. He had nothing but his fists, but he knew how to

use them. With barely time to brace himself he drove a
short right at the charging fisherman's jaw. His knuckles
found their mark, and the man's own momentum gave
the blow such terrific impact that he spun like a top and
fell face down in the sand.

Jim did not wait for him to rise. With panting haste
he ran the dinghy into the waves and leaped aboard.
Before the second man could join the attack he was out
of reach and rowing with all the strength of his arms.

XII

EALIZING that if the shrimpers fol-
lowed him in their sailboats he might
be easily overtaken, Jim did not head
out into the sound, but kept his course
parallel with the shore and pulled his
hardest. He could see men running to and fro on the pier,
small as ants in the distance, and expected momentarily
to see a sail run up on one of the fishing craft. But the
minutes passed and still no sign of pursuit became visible.
At last he leaned on his oars, gasping with weariness. He
had rowed nearly a mile at top speed. To the boy's exhaustion was added a heartsick sense of loneliness. He
was an outcast—he and his dog. At any rate he had
Dodo, and it made him feel better to see the courageous
little spaniel licking busily at his wounded shoulder, apparently undaunted by his encounter.

Jim grinned at him. "Folks don't seem so anxious to

make friends with us, dog," he panted. "Must be something wrong with us—the color of our hair, maybe."

The spaniel's tail wagged sympathetically and he jumped down from the stern thwart to put a moist nose against Jim's hand.

"Huh!" chuckled the boy, "I'll bet if there was any way you could pull an oar you'd help get us out o' this scrape." And so saying, he bent his back to the job again.

In spite of the fact that none of the fishermen's boats had put out after him, Jim could not get over the feeling that he was still in danger. As he rowed, he continually turned his head landward to watch for possible pursuers. But there was no movement in the sinister green of the jungle except the occasional flight of a bird.

The wind held steady from the south and he had to pull extra hard on his starboard oar to keep from being driven inshore. As it was, his course was rarely more than a quarter of a mile from the beach. By midday he realized that he was growing faint with hunger and that he must stop and eat soon if he was to have strength enough to go on. He had been rowing nearly four hours, and the fishing village lay so far behind that the pier was no more than a blur on the horizon. The duck he had killed that morning lay in the bottom of the boat, tempting his appetite. Finally he judged it safe to land. He took a long look at the shore, then swung the bow over and made for the beach.

The prospect of rest and food was cheering to Jim's

spirits. He even started to whistle a tune, but at a sudden movement from the spaniel the notes died on his lips. The dog's back was bristling and a low growl rumbled in his throat. He was looking at something that Jim, facing toward the stern, could not see. Swiftly the boy backed water with both oars and turned his head. He was within a hundred yards of the beach, but to his straining eyes there was nothing there but the narrow line of the sand and the rustling jungle.

"What's the matter with you, Dodo?" he asked, puzzled. "That little scrap must have made you nervous!"

The dog's answer was a louder growl that ended in an explosion of excited barking.

"All right then, boy," said Jim. "I'll take your word for it. We'll make our landing somewhere else."

He pulled the boat around and was starting to row on westward when there came a shout from the beach and two men burst out of the thicket. One of them was leveling a gun. Jim shot the boat out from shore with one powerful stroke and then ducked below the gunwale. Crouching there, he heard the crack of the report and with it the scream of the ball, close to his ear. When he lifted his head for another look he saw that only one of his enemies was armed. The other was shaking his fists with rage while his companion hastily reloaded.

Jim jumped back to the thwart and had time for a dozen quick strokes before the weapon was aimed again. This time the bullet imbedded itself with a thud in the thick oak planks of the dinghy's stern. And Jim had taken the boat well out of range by the time the angry shrimper was ready for a third shot.

The boy kept on rowing till he was half a mile from shore. There he knew he was safe, for the time at least, and able to take some sorely needed rest. Letting the boat drift, he dug under the stern thwart and brought out the three crabs he had cooked the day before and the water-filled calabash. The food and drink did him good. He ate slowly, taking an occasional pull at the oars to keep his distance from the beach, and talking to Dodo as he fed him with choice scraps.

"That sure was a good job," he told the dog. "Guess I wouldn't be here now if you hadn't let me know about those rascals. They were ready to drill me right through the back."

After an hour's respite, Jim pushed on. He watched the beach narrowly for some sign of his pursuers, but if they were still on his track they kept out of sight. The shore line now was more and more irregular, broken by islands and marshy coves, and this cheered the boy, for he knew the shrimpers would have difficulty in following him.

At last, shortly before sunset, Jim sighted another wide bayou mouth. From point to point spread at least a mile of open water, and he could see that it extended far inland. Jim had considered the possibility of drifting all night in the dinghy, but now it seemed no longer needful. He rested on his oars and took counsel with himself. Surely the shrimpers would have to turn back at the bayou, unless they had some sort of boat concealed there. And even so he doubted if their desire for vengeance would keep them on the trail after nightfall.

He rowed on through the gradually deepening dusk and landed in a sheltered cove some distance beyond the bayou. It seemed wiser not to risk lighting a fire that night, even though it meant going to bed supperless. Jim carefully primed his musket and placed it within reach of his hand. Then, with the keen-eared little dog curled up beside him, he lay down in the shelter of the boat. For a while the rustle of the leaves and all the minute noises of the night kept him awake. But his body was too tired to resist sleep long. Before he knew it he was soundly slumbering.

It was daylight when the cold touch of the spaniel's nose on his face woke him. He sprang up, fearful of an attack, but the beach drowsed in the morning light, and all was just as he had left it. Jim soon had a fire going and proceeded to clean and cook the duck as before. While his roast was simmering he prowled along the shore of the cove with his gun, hoping to surprise some sort of game.

There was a strange quiet over everything that morning. It gave the boy an uneasy feeling that he could not shake off. Not a bird sang in the thicket. Not a bright wing fluttered amid the still, green leaves. Jim stood awhile, puzzled by this sudden disappearance of the wild life of the shore. Finally he shook his head and spoke to Dodo. "All I can think of, dog," he chuckled, "is that the birds up here have heard how I can shoot."

They walked on, and at the head of the cove, in a pool of shallow water, Jim found some crabs. He had kept the shoestring crab line in his pocket. At the end of half an hour's fishing he had landed a round dozen of the voracious brutes, all of fair size. The duck, he knew, would have to cook for several hours; so he heated stones preparatory to steaming the crabs in seaweed. Prudently he decided to take the crabmeat out of the shells and save it for emergency rations.

Out of a handful of tough, broad leaves and some pliant stems of creepers he fashioned a sort of pouch, crude but serviceable, to hold the meat. By the time this container was finished to his satisfaction and he had packed it full of the white flakes of cooked crab, the morning was nearly gone.

Jim had been too deeply occupied to look about him much during the last hour or two. Now, as he glanced at the sky, he realized that its appearance had changed since dawn. The light haze that had hung over the sound had thickened to a dingy gray. The air had a still, oppressive heaviness.

"I don't like the looks of it much, Dodo," he told the dog. "We'd better get on our way before it starts to rain."

The duck was well roasted by this time. They finished it between them and pushed off again in the boat shortly after noon.

It was Jim's idea to go on up the shore a few more miles till he found some sheltered place where he could haul out the dinghy and make a snug nest under it during the rain. For rain was coming, he was sure. Meanwhile, however, he found the rowing easy, for the water was curiously smooth.

He had made perhaps two miles to the westward when the stillness of the sea and sky underwent a subtle change. It was not a noise that reached the boy in the boat, so much as a sudden pressure on his eardrums. Dodo felt it, too, for he shivered and whined. Off to the south Jim saw a dark line on the gray water, and it broadened even as he watched, advancing with incredible swiftness. The wind!

Expecting the approach of the storm, Jim had kept his boat within a few hundred yards of the shore. He turned now and pulled strongly for the beach, but the air was already filled with strange, whistling gusts, and the line of tortured water was gaining on him with appalling speed.

Fearfully he glanced over his shoulder. The sand and the bending trees were close. He wrenched at the oars with the strength of desperation, but the dinghy seemed to move at a snail's pace compared with the onrushing wall of water. Ten feet high it seemed to loom as it came toward him—a destroying avalanche of wind-driven sea.

Two more strokes and he could make it! One more! But even as he gave the final pull the crest of the great wave towered over him and fell. In that split second before the crash came, blotting out the world, Jim grasped instinctively at two things—his gun and his powder-flask. The next instant he was torn out of the boat and whirled up the beach under the crushing force of tons of water. Half drowned, the boy felt himself rolled over and over till his body struck against something solid. Then the wave washed back and left him, dizzy and choking, on the sand.

For a moment he was violently ill, but after getting rid of some of the salt water he had swallowed, he was able to sit up weakly and look about.

The hard object which he had been thrown against turned out to be a tree. He was far above the sand, in the edge of the woods. Stupidly he looked down at the musket and the flask of powder, still clutched fast in his hands. Where were Dodo and the boat, he wondered?

Struggling erect, he tried to launch a call into the screaming wind, but his voice was literally driven back down his throat. Twice he attempted walking, only to be swept off his feet by the force of the gale. The waves were still lashing far above the ordinary tide line, but there was a narrow stretch of spray-drenched beach, along which Jim started to crawl. Before he had gone ten feet his hand came in contact with something smooth and round, half buried in the sand. It was the water-gourd, washed up by that first huge wave. To his joy, the stopper was still tightly in place.

Almost at the same moment Jim saw the wreck of what had been his boat, wallowing in the furious seas just below him. It was upside-down, and the waves were pouring in and out of huge gaps smashed in its bottom. Suddenly, alongside the battered hulk appeared a strange-looking animal, struggling up the beach out of the raging water.

Jim, still dull-witted from the pounding he had received, stared at it open-mouthed. And not till the beast was almost in front of him did he realize that it was Dodo, wet and bedraggled, but proudly bearing the bundle of crabmeat in his mouth. The little dog staggered in the wind, and Jim clutched him tight before he could be blown away.

Then came the rain—such rain as Jim had never seen before. It drove in blinding sheets across the sound, riding the full blast of the hurricane. It beat on the boy and the dog as if it would force them deep into the sand. Jim gathered up the calabash, the gun, and the powder-flask.

"Come on, Dodo," he gasped, and crept toward the trees. In a moment he and the dog had slipped through a gap in the tattered mass of creepers and were sheltered from the fiercest onslaught of the rain.

There they huddled and waited. There was nothing else they could do—no other place to go. Jim held the small, shivering spaniel against his breast and meditated grimly on their situation. The loss of the dinghy was a bitter blow to him. He had counted on it to bring them close to New Orleans. Now they must make their way afoot, and he had seen enough of the coast to know something of the difficulties they might expect to encounter in that swampy network of bayou and forest.

Thanks to Dodo, they had food for a day or more, and if the rain ceased and gave him a chance to dry his powder he might kill some game with the musket. The shotpouch, still containing a dozen rounds of bullets, was in his pocket, where he had carried it from the start.

Jim had no way to estimate the passage of time, but at last, after what seemed an interminable while, he began to sense a slackening in the fury of the storm. He was cramped and cold from crouching so long in one position, and he could not possibly get any wetter than he was. There was a chance that if he went farther up the shore he might find more adequate shelter. He collected his gun and provisions, gave Dodo a pat of encouragement, and plunged out into the hurricane.

Though the wind still howled and the waves came smashing far up the beach, Jim found it possible now to keep his feet and struggle forward. It was exhausting work. In half an hour he advanced perhaps half a mile. At last, when he felt as if he could go no farther and was ready to crawl once more into the cover of the woods, he chanced to look ahead through the level streaks of rain

There, not above fifty yards from where he stood, the shore line curved sharply inward, and beyond it he saw a stretch of open water—evidently the mouth of a creek or bayou.

Jim pushed on, hoping that he might find a point of land with some sort of shelter in its lee. As they rounded the curve of the shore, the boy saw that he was on the margin of a wide river, stretching northward out of sight into the rain. There was nothing for it but to follow this east bank. Jim had taken half a dozen strides up the shore when he heard the bark of the spaniel behind him, faint in the wind. He turned to find the little dog jumping excitedly around a dark mass that lay in the wash of the waves.

At first the boy could not make out what the object was. Then he drew nearer, and a sickening feeling of recognition came over him. What he saw was not one dark mass but two—the naked bodies of two drowned negroes, chained leg to leg. Jim shuddered as he looked on this reminder of his days aboard the slaver. But he had not yet taken in the full significance of his discovery. On the beach, half hidden under the two corpses, and fastened to their fetters by a ring-bolt, was a long piece of broken plank. That could mean but one thing. These were not merely bodies of blacks who had died and been tossed overboard. Somewhere along the coast a slave-ship had gone ashore in the storm and pounded to pieces.

XIII

IM SLATER felt little inclination to linger there on the beach. Not only was he anxious to leave the scene of his revolting discovery as quickly as possible, but the vicious hammering of the wind and rain made it difficult to stay in one place even if he wished. He turned northward and made his way up the bayou shore. The gale pushed him along now, but there was no beach on which to walk. Jim and the dog were forced either to wade in the treacherous water close to the bank or to scramble among roots and vines.

At last they reached a place where the bayou made a sharp bend to the left and a thick cane brake lined its shore. But between the woods and the cane a sort of path had been beaten down by the wind, and Jim stumbled forward along this lane, looking always for a sheltered covert among the trees. Night, hastened by the storm, was already coming on.

Suddenly Jim found his feet squelching ankle-deep in water at each step. He plowed ahead, hoping to find firmer footing beyond, but the swamp only seemed to grow deeper. Baffled, he was about to start back, when Dodo gave a whine and crouched against his legs. There in the bent cane behind him Jim saw a movement— gliding, sinuous. He shivered as he realized how close he must have come to treading on the snake. With a sense of panic, the boy plunged to his right into the woods, hoping to find higher ground. There were root hummocks and fallen logs that lay above the level of the muck, but all around him, through the dark of the trees, he could see water glimmering. The swamp was everywhere.

At the end of a long search through the thicket Jim came to a fallen tree lodged across the roots of a big cypress. By sitting on the prostrate log with his back against the cypress trunk he was shielded somewhat from the wind. At first he was too chilled and dispirited to do anything but huddle there and hold the spaniel to his breast. In the stupor of fatigue and exposure that gripped him it hardly seemed to matter whether he lived or died.

But somewhere inside him a stubborn spark must have smoldered, for he roused himself after a time and fumbled beside the log till he found the pouch of crabmeat. "Come on, dog," he muttered in Dodo's ear. "What we need is probably something to eat."

With numb fingers he doled out a share of food for each of them. It was while they were eating that Jim noticed for the first time that the storm had slackened. Only an occasional puff of wind shook the rain down from the cypress tops, and the black of night had brought with it a breathless hush almost as oppressive as the one that had preceded the gale.

The dark was so intense that Jim could no longer see his hand when he moved it in front of his face. But though his eyes were of no use to him, his other senses were exceptionally alert. He could feel the spaniel moving close to his feet and hear him sniffing for possible stray morsels of food.

The forest was full of small noises. There was a constant drip and gurgle of water, a creak of branches as the trees stretched and straightened after the storm, and the soft, padding footfalls of small animals going about their hunting. Occasionally Dodo's body would stiffen at the sound of some stealthy movement, and once he barked sharply when a stricken rabbit screamed, far off in the woods.

Hunched on his log, Jim tried to sleep, but the memory of what he had seen on the beach came back to bother him. Not many slave-ships ventured into those closely-guarded waters. Could it be the *White Angel?* He wondered if poor Matt Beckett was warm at last. The boy was still turning the idea over in his mind when a sound startled him—a distant booming bellow that echoed menacingly across the swamp. Before Jim could collect his wits an answering roar came from his right, not twenty yards away. And as Dodo jumped, terrified, into his lap, there followed the scramble and splash of a big body sliding into the water.

The young Northerner had no way of knowing that what he had heard was the hoarse challenge of a bull alligator. All he could do was to sit there on the log and try to bolster his own courage by reassuring the frightened spaniel.

"It's all right, dog," he murmured through chattering teeth. "Whatever it was, it's not looking for us. See—it's gone now. Why, we're just as safe here as—as—well, anyhow, we're safe."

But he felt a little safer when he had drawn the long seaman's dirk out of its sheath and held the comforting weight of the hilt in his hand.

Jim's tense nerves must have relaxed at last. Hours later he opened his eyes to daylight and realized that he had been asleep. A terrible stiffness cramped his back and limbs, and he had to pound one leg a long time to get the numbness out of it. But when he lifted his head he could see bits of clear blue sky through the cypress tops. In sheer gladness at being alive he soon forgot to notice his aches.

Dodo, who had been out of sight in the woods when the boy awoke, came rushing back in answer to his whistle.

"Time to get moving, dog," Jim told him, and picked up the gun and the provisions. "Before we leave here, though," he added, "I'd like to take one peek at the place where we heard that noise."

A little distance to the eastward they came on a narrow, curving arm of the bayou. It looked black and uninviting. In the muck at its edge there was a broad trail where some big beast had gone wallowing into the water, but look as he would, Jim could see nothing of any animal that might have made it.

"No," he said, between relief and disappointment. "There's not a thing there but that old log."

Dodo did not agree with him, however. The dog advanced warily, with a series of short, excited barks, and when he was a dozen feet from the bank Jim saw the log move. A huge, gnarled head lifted at one end. The mouth opened just enough for him to see two long rows of terrible teeth, and shut silently again. Then the big 'gator swung lazily about and slipped into the bayou.

Jim had nearly fallen over backward when the great brute started to move. Now he stood with bulging eyes and watched the bubbles rise at the spot where it had disappeared. The spaniel had rushed to the bank in a frenzy of barking.

"You come here, Dodo, and stay close to me," Jim ordered soberly. "I guess maybe that was a crocodile or some such heathenish beast. But anyhow the place for us is somewhere else."

They picked their way northward among the trees, keeping to the hummocks as much as possible and wading only when they had to. Sparkling in the morning sun, the forest was a far pleasanter place than it had seemed in the dark and wet of the night before. Through the branches flitted little bright-feathered warblers of many hues, and the woods and canebrake were filled with singing.

For a mile or more Jim and his dog succeeded in threading through the swamp. Then they found themselves stopped by a loop of the bayou. The boy skirted its bank to the left, hoping to find another bend that would let them go forward. But beyond the edge of the cane the bayou curved south instead of north. Apparently there was no way around. Jim led the way back to the point of the bend and measured the width of the creek with his eye. At one spot it was hardly more than twenty feet across, but it looked dark and deep. He cut a long sapling and thrust one end down into the water. The depth was only four or five feet, but there was soft muck at the bottom that he did not like.

The boy cast a wary glance up and down the banks, for the memory of the moving log was still strong in him. At last he laughed at his own hesitation. "No sense in staying here," he told Dodo. "The longer we wait the worse it looks."

With careful aim he threw his precious gun to the opposite side, following it with the powder and shot, the calabash and the heavy knife. Then he took a short run and dove head first into the sluggish water. Three swift strokes and he was over, scrambling up the other bank. "Come on, dog," he called cheerfully and slapped his hands on his knees.

But Dodo stayed where he was. The little dog quivered and whined with the conflict between his fear and his anxiety to obey. He made quick dashes up and down the shore, hunting desperately for a way over, but born swimmer though he was, he seemed to distrust this particular stretch of bayou.

"All right," chuckled Jim, "I'll dry my clothes while you're getting up your courage." He stripped and spread his shirt and trousers in the sun. Then he turned his attention to the musket, swabbing out the rust and moisture and carefully wiping the lock. To his relief he found the powder dry in the tightly-stoppered flask, in spite of the constant wettings of the last twenty-four hours. When he had rammed home a charge and put fresh priming in the pan he began looking around for breakfast.

His eye fell on the spaniel, still waiting disconsolately on the other shore. "Look here, Dodo," he ordered. "No more fooling—come here, sir!"

There was a look of desperation in the dog's brown eyes that Jim was not soon to forget. He whimpered once, then gathered himself obediently and jumped. Even before he struck the water Jim tried to shout a warning. Out from the shelter of the farther bank he had seen a ripple move, and behind it, dimly outlined, the grizzly body of a ten-foot alligator.

Jim's gun was in his hands. He jerked it into position and fired point-blank at the horrible little turret-like eyes of the saurian. Thick smoke veiled the surface of the bayou for the next few seconds, and Jim could do nothing but wait, tense with apprehension. Then out of the clearing cloud, Dodo came scrambling up the bank to him, and beyond, in the creek, a great scaly tail thrashed furiously at the water. The boy caught a momentary glimpse of the wounded alligator's belly, and then it vanished in a swirl of bubbles, under a mass of floating water plants.

With the panting little dog in his arms, Jim retreated to the shade of a magnolia and sat down until his clothes had dried. "Well, we're all square, Dodo," he told the spaniel. "You got me into that mix-up with the shrimpers and then got me out again. This time it was my fault, dog, and I'm sorry. But anyhow you're safe."

Soon the sun had rendered his shirt and trousers wearable once more, and they resumed their journey. The ground on this side of the bayou was higher and less swampy, and there were open spaces in the woods that made the going easier. It was just as they were entering one of these grassy glades that Jim saw a movement at the edge of the trees opposite him. He stopped in his tracks and slowly raised the loaded gun. Almost hidden by the tall grass, a deer was feeding. Its head was out of sight, but Jim could see the red-brown back and the tail like a white handkerchief flicking upward at the flies.

The distance was close to the limit of his musket range —something over fifty yards. He waited, breathless, while the deer moved on, step by step. Finally he began to fear it would enter the woods without offering him a target, and he gave a quick, shrill whistle. At once a pair of big ears came into view, and the brown head of a doe, looking intently across the clearing.

Jim aimed a shade to the right and pulled the trigger. At the deer's wild leap he knew that once more his bullet had sped true. He ran through the grass and came on his quarry, not a dozen feet from where it had been standing. His heart smote him as he looked at the protruding tongue and pitifully glazing eyes. Still, he had killed for food, and there was no use in being sentimental about it. With his knife he made sure that the doe was past all suffering.

Within ten minutes Jim had a good fire burning, and half an hour later he was enjoying a venison steak, broiled on a green stick over the coals. There were little pools of fresh water left by the rain in every hollow in the woods. From one of these the boy refilled his cala-bash, and with several more pieces of cooked deermeat wrapped in leaves and bound into a bundle, he was ready for the trail again.

That was a pleasant day's travel. The hurricane had cleared and cooled the air, and if it had not been for the semi-tropical vegetation and the strange birds and beasts, Jim might have thought himself at home in Rhode Island on a fine June morning.

They were following the crest of a low ridge that seemed to divide two areas of tangled swamp. If they had struck inland a half mile to either side, their progress would have been made hopeless by canebrake and matted jungle. As it was, they moved through fairly open woodland, and Jim estimated they must have covered eight or nine miles to the northward by the time sunset came.

He made camp in a little glade where the big stars blazed through the tree-tops, and lay for a long time listening to the mysterious music of the southern night. In the dusk he thrilled to a sorrowful crooning that sounded like a whippoorwill's call but was somehow different. And afterward, when the moon rose, there came the loveliest song he had ever heard—the sweet, full-throated melody of a mocking-bird.

Jim was ready for rest, after his sleepless hours of the night before. And this time his slumbers were undisturbed.

The morning was fair and fine when he awoke. With Dodo he breakfasted on cold venison, and once more they took up their journey. Before they had gone a mile Jim found that they were following what seemed to be a faintly marked path through the woods. At first Jim thought he was merely walking along a deer trail, but soon he noticed a weathered ax-mark on the side of a tree, shoulder high, and he knew that men had blazed the way. Dodo, sniffing eagerly along the trail, showed by his actions that he, too, knew civilization was near. With a feeling of expectation, the boy pushed forward, and he was not surprised when suddenly they came out on a road. It was rough and grass-grown, but there were well-worn wheel-ruts that told of recent use.

"Let's see," said Jim; "it runs east and west. If I've been figuring right, New Orleans is west of us."

And without more hesitation he turned to the left.

XIV

HEN the boy and the dog had gone a mile or so along the cart-track, Dodo stopped and looked back, growling. Jim had learned caution from his experiences of the last few days. He slipped off the road into the brush and crouched there, holding the spaniel by the scruff of the neck. A moment later his ears, less keen than the dog's, caught a creaking rumble, and soon a wagon appeared, down the road to the eastward. It was a high, two-wheeled affair, drawn by a pair of shabby little brown mules that stepped along at a smart walk.

As the vehicle approached, the driver struck up a rollicking song in Creole French. He was a fat, round-faced little man, with sweeping black mustachios and a wide-brimmed straw hat that shaded him like an umbrella. When the team was almost abreast Jim stepped out of the bushes.

"*Mille tonnerres!*" cried the little man, and hauled back on the reins so violently, in his surprise, that the mules almost sat down. Then he reached for his stick and would have whipped the beasts to headlong flight if Jim had not thrown down his gun and held up his hand in a friendly salute.

"Hold on!" he laughed. "I don't want to hurt anybody. Does this road go to New Orleans?"

The Creole understood his pointing gesture and nodded vigorously. Then he looked a second time at the smiling, freckled countenance of the big Yankee lad and seemed to be reassured. He moved over on the crude seat of the cart.

"Come," he said. "I carr' you dere, eh? Me, I t'ought first you was robber—pirate, maybe. Ha, ha!"

Jim laid his musket and other belongings on top of the loaded cart and climbed to the seat beside the driver. The little Frenchman whipped up his team and they proceeded, with Dodo trotting beside the wheel.

"How far is it to the city?" the boy asked.

"Oh, maybe t'ree—four hour we come dere," replied the teamster.

Jim, raised in a part of the country where all the hauling was done by horses and oxen, was curious about the animals in front of him. "Are those mules?" he asked.

The Creole stared at him in blank amazement. *"Diable!"* he exclaimed. "W'ere you come from, eh? Don' you never see mules?"

Jim told him something about Rhode Island and

briefly sketched the adventures that had brought him so far from home. The Frenchman nodded and clucked in sympathy as the narrative progressed, and put in frequent comments of his own. *"Ah, oui,"* he said, "dose shrimpers, dey're bad feller. Don't do not'ing but fight an' steal. Now tell me, wot you do w'en you come to New Orleans, eh?"

"Well," Jim answered, "I figure to find a berth aboard a ship bound back to Boston or New York, and work my passage. Or I might go up river on a steamboat to Pittsburgh, and get home that way."

When noon arrived the driver halted his team in a shady place and produced a flagon of sour white wine and some bread and cheese. Jim brought out the remainder of his venison and traded a part of the meat for a chunk of dark bread that tasted delicious after his forced diet of the past five days.

Soon after they resumed their journey the cart-track on which they had been traveling joined a broader and better-made road. Other farmer's wagons appeared ahead of them, and to the west, Jim could see the smoke of the city. The road led them across a great low marsh on a corduroy causeway of logs, and on the farther side scattered shanties came into view.

A few minutes more and the town was all about them. They passed the Congo Square, a great, bare field, its floor of earth hard-trampled by the feet of countless negroes in their weird night dances. Beyond, they came through squalid streets to the old French Market. Now, in the heat of the afternoon, it was deserted save for such farmers as were bringing in their fruit and vegetables and fowls, or merchants getting ready for the morrow's selling.

Jim helped the Creole unload his produce at a market stall and thanked him for the ride. "Can you tell me," he asked, "how to find the Little Rue St. Jean? I have an errand there."

"*Mais, oui!*" exclaimed the voluble little man. "It is a fine street of rich houses." And with much gesticulating and drawing of airy diagrams he showed the boy how it might be reached.

Jim bade him farewell and set out up one of the little, ill-paved streets of the Creole quarter. He still carried his musket and powder-flask, his big calabash, and at his hip the long-bladed knife of Pedro, the pirate. His face and arms were weathered to a brick brown and his hair bleached by the sun. At his heels trotted the spaniel, no longer silken-coated but so dirty and unkempt that it would have been hard to name his breed. Small wonder that peals of half-smothered laughter rang from iron balconies above his head as Jim tramped along the *ban-quette*.

After many turnings he arrived at last at his destination. There was no need to ask which of the mellow old brick houses was that of Madame LeGros. Dodo gave a joyful bark as they entered the street, and frisked ahead to stand expectantly before a wrought-iron gateway in a high, vine-covered wall. Jim joined him there in a moment and pulled lustily at a ring-shaped handle which caused a bell to tinkle on the other side of the grill. Its echoes died away and everything became still—so still that Jim could hear the long grass rustle in the garden. He waited several minutes and pulled again, harder, but there was no answering footfall on the brick path. Backing off, he looked at the upper stories that showed above the wall, and noticed for the first time that all the windows were tightly shuttered.

When the boy knocked at the door of a neighboring house he was met by a colored serving-woman who looked suspiciously at his clothes and finally vouchsafed the information that "M'ame LeGros, she done gone a-visitin' to some plantation up de ribber."

Jim shouldered his possessions once more and started down the street. It was not until he reached the corner that he discovered Dodo was not with him. Looking back, he saw the little dog sitting patiently in front of the iron grill of the LeGros mansion. The boy whistled and called him by name, but Dodo remained immovable. Even when Jim went back and coaxed him, it was useless. The spaniel's tail dusted the pavement and he licked Jim's hand eagerly, but in his distressed brown eyes was devotion to duty. The boy could see at a glance that, short of dragging Dodo away by force, it would be impossible to move him.

"All right, dog," he said at length. "You're probably right, but I sure am going to miss you. I'll come back later and see if you've changed your mind."

The little dog whined as if he understood, and Jim turned regretfully away.

Though he knew little of the city's geography, the boy was able to lay his course for the water front without much difficulty. Over the roofs he caught repeated glimpses of ship masts and rigging, and toward these he bent his steps. Used as he was to the shipping in the port of Providence, it was a very different sight that now met his eyes.

Instead of descending to the docks, the land actually rose a dozen feet or more to the top of the levee. Behind the broad embankment, rows of taverns, warehouses, and shipchandlers' shops jostled each other for room on a muddy thoroughfare that lay far below the level of the river.

Jim climbed the levee and strolled along it, zigzagging among the piles of cotton bales, molasses hogsheads, and other merchandise that crowded its expanse. It was now nearly six o'clock in the evening and there was little movement on the levee. Only at one spot, some distance upstream, was there an appearance of activity. There a big ship, deeply laden, was taking on the last of her cargo. As Jim approached, he saw a small army of sweating negroes rushing bales and boxes aboard. A burly mate

stood beside the gangplank and cursed them with me-
thodical thoroughness as they worked.

With some diffidence, Jim addressed this formidable
personage. "Sailing tonight?" he asked.

"Ay," roared the officer, "if these black-skinned
blighters'll move their feet, we'll be sailin' to catch the
next tide."

"Where are you bound?" asked the boy.

"Liverpool's our home port, but we'll be stoppin' at
Baltimore to discharge some cargo on the way."

Jim screwed his courage a notch higher. "Could you
use another foremast hand—as far as Baltimore?" he
gulped.

For the first time the mate turned from the work in
hand and looked at him. His face was purple with rage.
"Why, you blankety-blank river rat!" he yelled. "Do ye
think we've got deck space for every lubber of a flatboat-
steerer as wants to get home?"

Jim straightened. "I'm no river rat," he said. "I'm a
deep-water sailor, out of Providence."

The mate looked him up and down, a trifle less scorn-
fully. "Ye're big an' strong enough," he admitted, "but
even if ye were a real A.B. we're overmanned as it is.
Anyhow, the skipper's ashore an' won't be back for an
hour or two. He holds no love for Yankees, but it
wouldn't do much harm to ask him before we sail. Here,
ye flat-footed loafers, get your backs into it!" And he
turned to the line of stevedores once more.

Jim thanked him and wandered on. He had small hope of getting a berth on the lime-juicer, but the attempt was worth making. Meanwhile he had some time to kill, and there was a chance that he might hear news of other vessels soon to sail. He went down from the levee and headed for one of the largest of the waterside taverns.

Inside, a big whale-oil lamp burned, throwing a jumble of sharp lights and grotesque shadows about the wide, low-ceilinged room. There must have been a hundred men lined up along the bar or seated at little board tables. The place was thick with smells, the most dominant of which seemed to be pipe-smoke and the fumes of raw whisky. This was no Creole wine-shop but a rendezvous of sailors and river men who liked their liquor strong.

Never in his life had Jim seen such an assortment of races and types. There were raftsmen and broadhorn steerers in butternut brown; lean Tennessee backwoodsmen in buckskin leggings and linen hunting-shirts; tow-headed Danes and Swedes and ruddy-faced Britishers from the ships, and big-boned Ohioans from the river steamboats.

Jim hesitated a moment on the threshold, confused by the din of songs and rough laughter that filled the tavern. Then he edged his way along the sandy floor to a place behind one of the tables where he could overhear some of the talk that was going on. There were four men at the table. Three of them were ordinary seamen in

nondescript clothing, lolling over their glasses of grog.
But the fourth struck Jim at once as of a different stripe.
He was a stockily-built tar in the trim uniform and var-
nished black hat of the United States Navy. He leaned
back at ease and talked with the loud assurance of a man
well along in his cups. From time to time he reached up
to stroke a big green parrot that perched on his shoulder.

"We caught 'em comin' out of Mississippi Sound right
after sunrise," he was saying. "We knew that little black
schooner well an' knew she could outfoot us if she got
the wind on her quarter. But before old Yellow Beard
could get his topsails set we were up abeam and gave
him our starboard battery. I was pointin' the Number
Two gun, an' it was my chain-shot that carried away her
foremast just below the cross-trees. After that it was
easy. Wasn't it, Polly—eh?" He looked up at the parrot, which tweaked his ear and swore roundly that it was.

"I was in the first boat that boarded. We were over
the schooner's side without a man lost, an' we'd laid four
o' the pirates cold before they could give us a volley or
get their cutlasses in action. I jumped up on the quarter-
deck an' come face to face with the skipper himself—
Yellow Beard. I'd fired my musket an' hadn't had time
to load, but there he was a-swingin' his hanger at my
head. So what did I do but up with the butt o' the gun
like this—" He sprang to his feet and picked up his chair,
while the parrot teetered and scolded on his shoulder.

As the doughty sailor looked about for a target he

spied Jim standing against the wall. "Like this—" he repeated, and dropping the chair once more he snatched the musket from the hand of the startled boy and whirled it above his head. With a crash he brought the stock of the clubbed gun down on the table.

"I bashed his crown an' felled him like an ox!" the tar concluded triumphantly.

Jim took a quick stride forward, too angry to care about consequences. "Give me that gun," he said. "What do you mean by handling it that way? Look—you've smashed the lock!"

Lured by the sounds of an altercation, a crowd of spectators was gathering about the table. As Jim put out his hand for the musket the sailor pulled it back, out of reach.

"Avast there, my hearty!" he laughed. "Not so quick on the trigger. Just who might you be, anyhow?"

"Never mind who I am," Jim retorted. "That's my musket you've ruined with your horseplay. Now give it to me."

"The young stranger has plenty o' spirit," said the tar, leering around at the bystanders. "Ruined it, have I?" and he lifted the gun to examine the broken lock. Suddenly the expression on his flushed face underwent a change. He stepped nearer the lamp and bent, peering closely at the weapon. Then he turned swiftly on Jim.

"Aha, my fine lad!" he cried. "So that's where I've seen you afore! I thought them blue-striped pants had a mighty familiar cut to 'em. Look 'ee here, mates. The gun's got Yellow Beard's own mark on the stock—the skull an' bones an' the double B!" As the crowd edged closer the fellow pointed excitedly to a pair of small characters, burned with a hot iron into the underside of the stock, where Jim had never noticed them.

"Hold him, men!" bellowed the sailor. "He's one o' the three rascals that got away from us in a smallboat when the rest o' the gang surrendered. A bloody buccaneer—that's what he is!"

And above the ensuing din the dazed Yankee boy heard the parrot screaming, "Ay, ay—a blankety-blank bloody buccaneer!"

XV

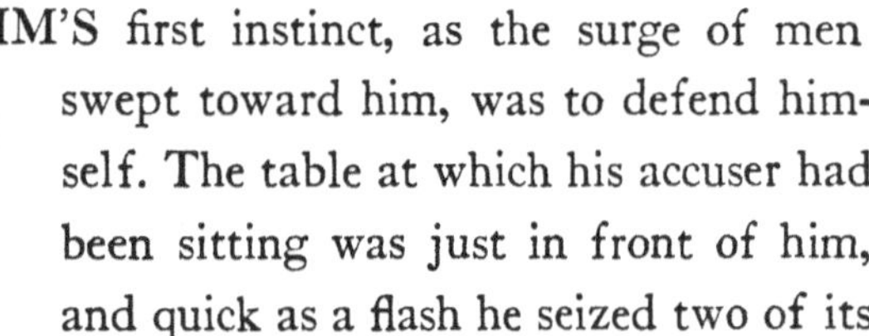IM'S first instinct, as the surge of men swept toward him, was to defend himself. The table at which his accuser had been sitting was just in front of him, and quick as a flash he seized two of its legs, jerking them upward. With the table tipped on edge, the top made a waist-high wall in front of him, and the legs gave him momentary protection from either side. Then with a rush the attacking mob was on him and he was lashing out with his fists at every face that came within reach.

For seconds that seemed like hours the boy kept up the hopeless battle. Finally something hard and heavy crashed against his head, and the room dissolved in a red blur of blows.

The next thing Jim remembered was a whistle, long and shrill. "The police!" a voice shouted, and there was a hurried shuffle of feet. He raised himself painfully on one elbow and looked about with dizzy eyes. He was lying, he discovered, on the sanded floor of the tavern.

WITH A RUSH THE ATTACKING MOB WAS ON HIM

Four men in strange, ornate uniforms, carrying drawn swords, had entered the barroom, and the crowd had drawn back, leaving an empty space, in the middle of which he lay.

The gun-pointer from the cutter was talking now. "This young devil is one o' Yellow Beard's crew," he bawled excitedly. "Here's his gun with the pirate marks on it. I disarmed the fellow myself."

Somebody guffawed at this, and the sailor bristled angrily. "He's my prisoner," he asserted. "Tie him up an' I'll see that he's turned over to the naval authorities an' properly hanged."

"Ay, that's the talk," some of the sailors shouted. "String him up—the dirty pirate!"

But the policemen had a different idea. Their leader was a fiery little Frenchman. "Not so!" he cried. "This brawl is a matter for the justice of the city. We will arrest him—thus—" He laid a hand on Jim's shoulder. "We will place him in the calaboza. He will be tried in due course."

There was a howl of derision from some of the onlookers, but mingled with it were shouts of approval. The river men were no special friends of the police, but they were always ready for a quarrel with the salt-water sailors. Half a dozen flatboat men stepped forward belligerently.

"Sure," they cried. "The kid put up a good fight. Give him his chance."

At this evidence of support, the policemen assumed an even more martial bearing. Two of them seized Jim by the arms and lifted him to his feet. He still swayed a little when he tried to stand, but his head was clearing fast.

"*Allons!* March!" ordered the doughty Creole officer with a twirl of his mustache, and at a smart parade step the squad moved out of the tavern.

The fresh evening air was a welcome change from the stuffy heat of the bar. Almost at once Jim felt his strength coming back, and though his head still throbbed he was able to think with some degree of coolness. After the threat of the seamen to hang him out of hand, he felt almost grateful for his present predicament. And yet, as he well knew, it would be hard for him to prove his innocence before a court of law—especially since, for all he knew, the trial might be conducted in French. His heart sank as he thought how solid the chain of evidence against him would look to a hostile jury.

The gendarmes were leading him through a small, unlighted street—probably a short cut, he thought, on the way to the jail.

Suddenly there was a shout, and out of a narrow alley beside them poured five or six shadowy figures. The two policemen who gripped Jim's arms broke into a run and hustled him with them up the street. Meanwhile the others blew furious blasts on their whistles and laid about them with their swords.

Looking back over his shoulder, the boy saw one of the Creole officers trip and fall under the blows of his assailants. Then there was a heavy pounding of feet close behind them, and the two panting gendarmes let go Jim's arms and turned to defend themselves. For a second the boy stood irresolute. He thought he was being rescued, though who his deliverers might be he did not know. Then he saw the dark silhouette of the gunner's hat and realized in a flash that he was in greater danger than ever. At that very instant one of the sailors lunged forward, hands outstretched to seize him. But Jim dodged in time. Twisting like an eel, he ducked under the fellow's arm and doubled back down the street.

In the dark the struggling group by the alley failed to see him until he was past them and away. Barefooted, he sped like a silent wraith to the end of the dark street. There he crossed a wider thoroughfare, ran along its farther side for a hundred feet, and dove into a little black lane between two warehouses before his pursuers had even reached the corner.

It was so dark in his retreat that for a moment he thought he was pocketed in a blind alley from which there was no exit. But as he felt his way along, a gray glimmer became visible at the farther end. He found that the passage made a bend to the left and then went on again, still between high, windowless walls. Now he could see a rectangle of sky ahead. He dashed on, stumbling through mud and refuse, and as he reached the end of the alley a sound of many voices broke out behind him. The pack was on his trail, in full cry.

Like a hunted fox, he stood gasping by the alley wall and looked out on the dark water front. At the moment there was no one in sight. He gathered himself together and darted across to the slope of the levee. At the top, in the friendly shelter of the huge piles of merchandise, he felt that he had a chance. It would be a minute or two before his pursuers came out of the alley.

With what breath remained to him Jim dashed up the levee, dodging in and out among the heaps of freight. There were inviting dark crannies between the hogsheads and barrels where he might have taken cover, but he ran on, intent on getting as far as possible before he was forced to hide. Suddenly, not fifty yards ahead, he saw a lantern bobbing. A levee watchman! The boy stopped running and huddled close in the shadow of a double tier of cotton bales, looking about for a place of conceal-ment. The man with the lantern was walking in his direction, and now from behind him he could hear distant shouting.

Jim felt with his hands along the pile of bales and discovered a foot-wide crevice in the upper row. It took him but a few seconds to pull himself up and work his legs and body into the opening. By doubling his knees he found he could get far enough in so that even his face was a foot or two back from the edge of the tier. With quick fingers he pulled handfuls of loose cotton out of the nearest bale and sprinkled it over his back and head. Then he lay still.

He did not have long to wait. The watchman had evidently heard the outcry from down the levee and Jim saw the flash of the lantern as he went past at a run. An interval of silence followed. Then came voices, half heard at first, but gradually growing louder.

Shadowy figures passed, accompanied by the lantern-bearer. A chill went through Jim when two men came to a stop directly in front of his crevice. He could have touched them merely by stretching out his hand. They were out of breath and panting.

"I'm quittin' right now," said one. "I've got a kink in me side already from chasin' the beggar."

"Wot makes 'em think he came this way?" asked the other. "He's likely a mile off down the levee by now."

"Yes, an' then he might be hid any place around here," returned the first speaker. He rested a hand on the edge of Jim's bale and appeared to be looking directly at him in the uncertain darkness. The boy broke into a cold sweat. He had to steel his nerves to keep from trembling. Then with a yawn the sailor turned away.

"Ho, hum!" he muttered. "If those fool police hadn't stuck their noses in, we'd ha' had him swingin' by now. Come on, Bill. I left a good half pint o' grog on the table in that tavern."

Not until the sound of their footsteps had wholly died away did Jim dare to draw a real breath. Cautiously he moved first one leg and then the other till he worked himself into a more comfortable position. He was very tired and his bruises were stiffening.

The other searchers must have gone on still farther and given up the chase, for he heard no more of them. From far away behind him came faintly the noises of the town, and nearer at hand the cluck and gurgle of the river. By raising his head Jim could see a steamboat moored almost in front of his hiding-place. Her twin stacks stood tall and black against the sky.

Once, when the minutes had dragged into hours, he saw a flicker of light and the watchman passed by, making his rounds. After that he saw nothing, for sleep overcame him.

The darkness was just beginning to thin into dawn when Jim awoke. A gray mist had risen from the river and hung shroudlike over the levee, and from the silence it appeared that no one was yet stirring in the town. Now, if ever, was the time to leave his hiding-place.

Painfully the boy moved his legs and arms, cramped from the position in which he had slept. The beating he had taken in the tavern was making itself felt now. He saw a dark stain on his shirt and realized that it was dried blood. Putting his hand to his temple he felt a deep, jagged cut there. It must have been a bottle that had struck him and knocked him out. A momentary faintness made him feel dizzy, but he waited, biting his lips, and it passed.

He looked out from the edge of the crevice. Nothing moved in the fog. He let himself down and slipped quickly across to another pile of freight nearer the water. From this point the steamboat was only a few yards away. Jim could see her deck, loaded high with sugar and cotton, and painted in great gilt letters on the pilot-house her name—"*Paragon*—Louisville."

The geography taught in the one-room schoolhouse back in Rhode Island had concerned itself very little with the American continent beyond the Alleghenies. Still, Jim had a hazy idea that Louisville was somewhere up the Ohio, in the general direction he wanted to go. The steamboat was deep-laden. She must, he thought, be nearly ready to sail. If he could get a job loading freight or stoking her boilers—but no, that wouldn't do. Some member of the crew would be too likely to recognize him. The boy still felt shaky when he remembered how close he had come to hanging the night before. His best chance of escape would be to stow away on the *Paragon* and hope to keep out of sight until the steamboat's paddles had put a sufficient distance between him and New Orleans.

As he crouched there, chilled by the morning mist, he heard a faint sound, close by on the levee. Some one was coming. Jim looked about in desperation for another hiding-place, but none was to be seen. He cowered back in the shadow of a big molasses hogshead and waited.

Then the intruder appeared. It was a little brown dog, padding along the levee, nose to the ground.

"Dodo!" Jim gasped, his voice shaking with relief. "Come here, dog!"

The spaniel heard him and raced to his side. "Quiet, boy—quiet!" breathed Jim. And Dodo seemed to understand, for he contented himself with frisking up and down and licking the lad's hands.

It was rapidly growing lighter. Jim made another cautious survey and picked the dog up in his arms. "If we're going aboard we've got to do it now," he murmured. "So don't you dare to bark, whatever happens." Furtively he dodged across to the edge of the levee and along the narrow plank that led to the bow of the boat. Once on her deck, he burrowed his way between two bales of cotton and dragged Dodo in after him. By shoving this way and that with his shoulders he was able to make a fairly comfortable nest. There was room to sit or lie down if he kept his knees curled up. The overhanging bales shielded him from above, and the opening by which he had entered was so small that only by bending almost to the level of the deck could any one see into it.

Jim had been none too quick in getting aboard. Scarcely had he settled himself and the dog when there was a clumping of boots on the deck and some one shouted an order. "Come on, Mike, get those fires up," another voice called. "We're due to start by sunrise."

There was a clang of iron furnace-doors and a smell of wood-smoke. Jim had never been aboard a steamboat before, but he had heard many stories of their speed and had some idea of the way they worked. He figured the crew must be throwing wood on the blaze beneath the boilers now.

Close by his nest on the fore deck, he could hear sharp commands given and the thud of bare feet as the deck-hands made final preparations for casting loose. Finally a bell clanged.

"How's your steam?" came a call from above, in the pilot-house.

"Hundred an' twenty. What d'ye say?" was the answer from somewhere aft.

"All clear astarn. Let her go!" bellowed the captain.

There was a creak and a rumble and a wheeze of steam. The big side-paddles churned the water slowly, and Jim felt the *Paragon* moving, backing her way out into the current of the Mississippi.

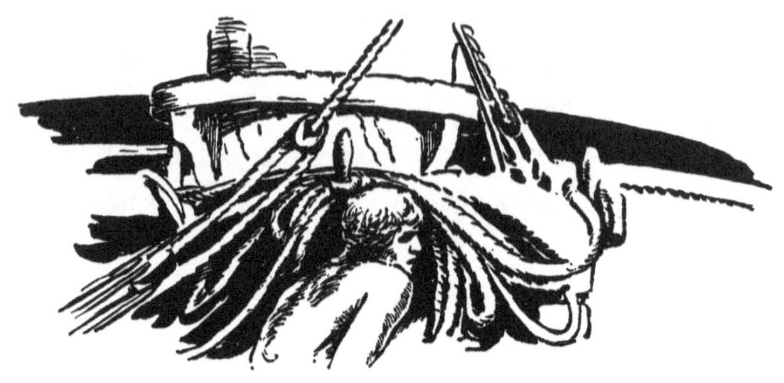

XVI

 LONG day began for Jim and Dodo. Wedged in their dark little world of ginned cotton and burlap, they had no choice but to listen and wait. As the sun rose higher it beat fiercely down on the loaded fore deck of the river boat. Before long the heat had penetrated to the cramped quarters where the two stowaways lay, and their discomfort was increased. Jim had lost his water-gourd, along with his gun, in the fight at the tavern. For twenty hours neither food nor water had passed his lips, and thirst made his mouth taste dry and cottony. The wound in his head throbbed with a feverish rhythm.

Stubbornly the boy refused to think about these difficulties. He was headed north. That was the main thing. With a steady splash of paddle-wheels, the steamer was pushing her way upstream. Occasionally the weird harmony of negro singing came to Jim's ears. There must be slaves aboard, bound for the up-river plantations. Once he heard the well-bred, silvery laughter of a lady passenger, from somewhere on the upper deck.

The *Paragon* made frequent stops at landings along the river. Sometimes Jim could tell by the rumble of rolling barrels that freight was being discharged or taken aboard. Other stops seemed to be for the purpose of loading wood for the ever-hungry fires.

There was no way for the boy to guess at the passage of time. Only from the faint light that came through the entrance to his cavern could he tell that it was still day. Dodo too must have been suffering from thirst, for after what seemed many hours he grew restless. Jim was forced to hold him by the scruff of the neck to keep him from going out on deck, and even so he could not stop the dog from uttering an occasional small, piteous whine.

It was after sunset when the steamer swung inshore with a banging of bells and stopped at another town. Jim guessed it to be a place of some importance, because the chatter and hum of a good-sized crowd came from the levee. He was not surprised when he heard one of the ship's officers call, "Here we are, folks—Donaldsonville. All ashore that took passage to Donaldsonville!"

The steamboat made a long stop here, for Donaldsonville, like Baton Rouge, Bayou Sara, and Natchez, was one of the principal river ports. After the passengers had disembarked and the crowd on the levee had gradually filtered away there was still a steady rumble of loading and unloading freight. But by the time darkness came, even these noises had ceased. Jim ventured to crawl to the opening of his den and look out. The deck, crowded with bales and barrels, was wholly quiet now. Jim waited a moment to make sure all the crew had gone ashore, then crept forth, with the eager Dodo pressing close at his heels.

When the boy stood erect he could see a group of deck hands and stevedores gathered on the landing under a sputtering oil flare. There was no chance of getting to the levee without being caught. Behind him he heard a low whine and found the spaniel crouched by the outer edge of the deck. There was no railing, and the muddy current ran past, only a scant two feet below. Jim caught the dog by the hind legs and let him down gently till his swollen tongue could reach the water. Dodo drank as if he could never get enough to quench his thirst. At last he gave a satisfied grunt and Jim hoisted him back to the deck.

Now it was the boy's turn. He moved aft to one of the upright pillars that supported the upper deck and twisted his legs around it. Then, hanging downward from the waist, he buried his face in the water. Never in his life had he been so grateful for a drink as he was for that deep draught of silt-laden Mississippi water.

Jim barely had time to pull himself up again when

he heard the captain's call of "All aboard!" Hurriedly he scuttled back to his hole under the bales and dragged Dodo in with him. They were barely in time, for a few seconds later there came a tramping of feet, and the deck hands returned to the boat. Then the engine bell jangled, and the *Paragon* got under way once more.

Through the night the boat steamed slowly. For a while Jim lay awake, listening to the droning voice of the leadsman at the bow, calling his soundings to the pilot. "Mark four!" he would shout. "Mark three! Quarter less three! Half twain! Half twain! Quarter twain! Mark twain! Mark twain!" And then, as the channel deepened again, "Half twain! Quarter less three! M-a-r-k three!"

The figures were given in fathoms, of course. Jim, accustomed to deep-draft sailing-ships, was still marveling at the fact that a big vessel like the *Paragon* could move along confidently in only twelve feet of water when he finally drowsed off.

All through that night and the next day the boy and his dog lay in their den beneath the cotton bales. Sometimes Jim dozed uneasily, but never for long. There was a dull ache of hunger in his stomach, and by sun-up he was suffering from thirst again. Just what he planned to do he did not know. His usually decisive mind seemed drugged by a mounting fever that came from the gash on his head.

Late in the afternoon of that second day something

happened that took the necessity of deciding out of the sick boy's hands. He had been asleep for a short time when he was roused by a sudden shout. Something was gripping his ankle. He struggled to free himself, still only half awake, and wrenched the dirk out of its sheath at his waist. Before he could gather his wits he was dragged out of the hole by strong hands and set roughly on his feet.

There he stood swaying weakly in the middle of a ring of deck hands—hard-bitten river men whose scowling faces held no friendliness. He heard Dodo whimper and saw the little dog in the grip of one of the steamboaters. Dully he realized that the spaniel must have stolen out in search of water and given their hiding-place away.

"Put up that knife!" growled one of the deck hands.

Jim looked down stupidly and found the dirk in his right fist. He replaced it in his belt.

"Could you—could I—get something to eat?" the boy asked thickly. "Or some water?"

"Huh!" said the man who had first spoken. "D'ye think this is a hotel?" He cupped his hands in the direction of the pilot-house. "Hey, Luke," he called. "Tell the cap'n we've got a stowaway."

"But I'll work—" Jim tried to tell them—"I want to work my way."

This brought forth nothing more than an ugly laugh

or two. "Yeah?" said one of the river men. "Looks like it—the way ye hid yerself."

The skipper of the *Paragon* appeared—a little red-faced man in blue coat and cap and an imposing double row of brass buttons.

"What's this?" he demanded. "Another loafer sneaked aboard? This him? Ha! A tough-lookin' customer, too."

Jim staggered forward eagerly. "All I want is to work my passage, sir," he pleaded. "I'm from New England —Providence—and I'm trying to get back home."

The captain gave little heed to this announcement. "Too many like you on the river," he snorted. "Every lousy flatboat hand thinks he's a steamboater when it comes time to go back where he came from. Ain't enough jobs for honest men, as it is."

"Luke!" he called to the pilot. "Head in for the nearest landin'. We don't need wood yet, but we can take on a couple o' cords and put this scalawag ashore."

"Next bend, above Bayou Jaune," replied the steersman, laconically.

The deck hands had dispersed at the arrival of the captain. Now, as he bustled away up the ladder, one of the crew strolled back toward Jim. He was a lean, stoop-shouldered man, with a comical lopsided grin and a lump in his gaunt cheek that marked the location of his quid of tobacco.

He spat casually in the direction of the rail, then spoke

in a low voice. "You from Providence, eh?" he said. "Born in Connecticut, m'self. Never went back sence I was a kid. B'en on the river twenty year." He paused and cast a careful eye about the deck.

"Reckon ye're purty dry after two days of it," he continued. "The water-bucket sets over yonder, behind them bales. Git yerself a drink 'fore they puts ye ashore. Soon's ye kin, I advise ye to have that head doctored. Wal—here's luck!"

Before Jim's groping brain could find the words to thank him, the fellow had walked away. It did not take the boy long to find the water-bucket. The stuff it held was tepid from sitting in the sun; yet to his feverish throat it gave a blessed relief. His legs were wabbly, and he sat down with his back against the bales. Slowly the laboring steamer swung across the current toward the right bank. Jim saw low woods fringing the shore and behind them a bluff rising steeply to rolling, forest-covered hills. It looked more like his own Rhode Island country than anything he had seen in his wanderings. Half delirious, he had a sense of coming home at last, and as the boat slid in crabwise toward the landing, he got unsteadily to his feet and stretched out his arms toward the trees.

When the *Paragon* was made fast, a couple of deck hands took the boy by the shoulders and hustled him from the deck to the flimsy landing-stage. Cordwood was piled close to the bank, and half a dozen roustabouts were already throwing it into a wide hatch amidships. Jim stood in a daze for several moments before he realized that Dodo was missing.

He tried to whistle, but his swollen, dry lips could not shape themselves to make the sound. Finally he succeeded in calling the dog's name, and on the deck of the steamer there was a sudden scuffle. One of the crew had liked the spaniel's looks and held on to him when Jim was put ashore. Now he let go with a howl of pain and swung his foot in a mighty kick that would have annihilated Dodo if it had caught him fair. But the dog was already scurrying for the rail. He jumped into the river, swam a dozen panting strokes to the shore, and came rushing, wet and draggled, to his master, while the river men laughed at their comrade's discomfiture.

The wood was soon loaded. One of the last of the crew to leave the landing as the vessel cast off was the Connecticut man. He looked at Jim and pointed up the shore. "There's a cabin up there," he shouted. "Reckon they'll take keer o' ye."

The boy watched the big paddles begin to churn as the *Paragon* headed her nose upstream once more. Then he started walking along the bank. There seemed to be no strength in his knees. Twice he sat down to rest before he came in sight of the bark roof of a crude little log house among the trees. There was no smoke coming from the chimney, and at first he thought there was no one at home. But when he knocked at the door it opened a crack. In the aperture he saw a thin, ragged little girl with a sallow face and scared eyes.

"Pappy ain't yere," she stammered, and would have shut the door in his face if he had not chanced to lurch against it at that moment.

"I'm sick," Jim said. "All I want is a little food, so I can get along further."

The child shook her head, terrified. "I cain't give ye nothin'! He'd lick me if'n I did," she whimpered. But the sight of the boy's stricken face must have moved her to pity. "Wait," she said finally, and disappeared into the dark interior of the cabin.

In a moment she was back with a dirty-looking piece of bread in her hand. "Here's some corn pone I was savin' fer supper," she murmured. "I had it hid in the ashes, but that'll bresh off. Thar's water back at the spring."

Jim thanked her and took the piece of corn bread. A little way behind the cabin he found the basin of a spring hollowed out of the hill. There he washed off the pone, drank again, and ate slowly, for at first he found it hard to swallow. It wasn't much of a meal, for he gave Dodo a fair share of it. But after a few minutes' rest he felt strong enough to go on. Returning to the cabin, he asked the little girl how far it was to the nearest town.

"Bayou Sara's yonder up the river a ways," she said. "An' thar's some big plantation-houses five or six mile

A TALL, STRONGLY BUILT MAN IN A BROWN
LINEN HUNTING-SHIRT

no'th of us. But ye cain't git to 'em 'thout climbin' the bluff, 'cause thar's swamps above yere."

"All right," answered Jim. "I'm mightily obliged to you. And I hope you don't have to go without your supper."

He went slowly back to the foot of the slope and made ready to climb. It looked like an almost impossible task in his weakened condition. Thick brush and creepers covered the face of the bluff, and it loomed above him, forbiddingly steep. He labored upward a dozen yards and stopped to rest, the blood pounding in his ears. Dodo scurried around him as if to show how easy it was, then rushed back to lick his hand and look at him with anxious brown eyes. "We'll get there, dog," Jim smiled wearily. "Only you'll have to wait for me."

In a moment he struggled on a little distance and stopped to rest again. After three or four of these efforts he had forgotten everything except the delirious obsession that he must reach the top. "Here, Dodo," he panted, "what's the use of fooling this way? Come on— I'll make it this time or bust!" And with a spurt of feverish strength he went crashing upward, gripping at tree trunks, tearing through the vines. The impetus of his rush carried him over the crest, and he ran on blindly for a short distance. Then a root tripped him and he fell, stunned and gasping, on his face. A roaring filled his ears, and everything went black.

How long the boy lay unconscious he never knew. It

must have been an hour or more, for dusk was settling through the trees when he opened his eyes again. Dodo was barking furiously somewhere close by. Then the dog's yelps changed to an eager whining, and he rushed up to lick Jim's face. A voice spoke, gently, above him. He rolled over and looked up to see a tall, strongly built man in a brown linen hunting-shirt, leaning on a long-barreled gun.

"Aha—and now I see!" said the man. He had a pleasant, low voice with an accent faintly foreign. "So this is why you wanted me to come with you, little dog!"

XVII

IM lay on a blanket, spread over a bed of leaves, and looked out at a bright forest morning. Above him was the rough shelter of a pole lean-to, thatched with bark. Outside was a log fireplace full of smoldering ashes, and an iron rod on two crotched sticks that held a blackened tin pail. At a sort of work-bench made of the two halves of a split log, the roughly clad woodsman toiled and whistled. And Dodo, torn between two desires, rushed back and forth from his sick master to their new acquaintance.

Jim's fever was gone, and frequent drinks of warm broth, given him every hour or two through the night, had brought back a little of his strength. But he still felt so languid and tired that he was content to lie quiet for a while.

The man outside looked up from his work and grinned at him in friendly fashion. He had a lively face with a high-bridged aquiline nose and sparkling gray eyes. His long hair hung in careless brown waves to his shoulders, and he wore no hat. His lean, strong hands were so quick and graceful in their motions that Jim was fascinated as he watched them. Now for the moment they were quiet, resting on his hips.

"How do they call you, my boy, eh?" he asked.

"Jim Slater," Jim tried to say, but his voice was weak and husky.

The man nodded. "Don't try to talk now," he said. "Your name is James, eh? So is mine. John James— Jean Jacques, in the French. Suppose, then, you call me Jacques—I call you Jim. And the dog?"

"Dodo," the boy murmured.

Jacques squatted on his heels. "Here, Dodo," he called, and when the little dog came to him he felt of his long ears and scratched his matted coat. "A spaniel of good blood," he said approvingly. "We must wash him when we come to a stream. And you, too, Jim. That head of yours—it has a deep cut and will heal slowly. Now I must go back to work."

He went to a tarpaulin-covered case under the shelter and took out of it a flat board a yard long and more than two feet wide. On this he fastened a large sheet of paper, pinning it down securely with broad-headed tacks from his pocket. As Jim watched him, he returned to the work-bench, propped his board against it and began to draw, with quick, careful strokes of the pencil. His eyes were constantly darting from the paper to some object on the bench that Jim could not see. At last the boy's curiosity grew so strong that he lifted himself on one elbow and peered over the edge of the puncheon table.

What he saw was a bundle of black and white feathers—the body of a dead bird. It lay on its side with head and neck stretched out, and one long, graceful wing held up as if in flight by an ingenious tripod of sticks and string.

Jacques must have heard the movement behind him, for he swung toward Jim. "Lie down," he ordered. "How will you get well if you do not rest? Look—I will move my bird so that we can both see him. I shot him yesterday just before Dodo brought me to you. A Mississippi kite, and a beauty, too. See—his neck and breast and all his under parts are bluish white, his back and wings almost black. And the beak—curved, but not deeply hooked like the beaks of his cousins the hawks. I think I shall draw him in the air—so."

His skillful fingers moved over the paper and caught the sweep of the poised wing in a few deft lines. When the outline of the bird was fairly complete he began laying in color with bits of bright chalk. Occasionally he hummed or whistled a lively little tune.

For nearly an hour Jacques worked steadily at his drawing. Then he rose, stretching his arms, and laughed as he glanced at the invalid on the blanket.

"Already you are better," he said. "Do you know how you looked when I found you? Like a wounded pirate, about to die on a strange shore!"

The boy winced a little, remembering he still wore the pirate clothes that had earned him a broken head in New Orleans. He would have tried to explain his costume at once, but the woodsman went on, chuckling to himself.

"I cannot lend you a mirror," said he, "but I will make a small sketch instead—see?" Eagerly he took chalk and paper and drew a few quick lines. "There," he explained, "the red is this big gash in your forehead. Do you recognize yourself?"

Jim looked at the likeness in amazement. The eyes and mouth and tousled hair were his, but he could hardly believe that the gaunt, hollow-cheeked visage in the picture belonged to him.

"Wow!" he grinned. "Do I look as bad as that?"

Jacques nodded. "More food is what you need. I will build up the fire and heat some broth. Lucky that I had those rabbits, is it not?"

He picked up an ax and was about to split a pine stick into kindlings when he paused suddenly, listening, his head cocked on one side. "Sh!" he whispered. "A hen turkey calling, off there in the woods. Maybe we shall have meat for dinner!"

Silently he took the fowling-piece from its place in a corner of the lean-to and stole away into the brush. Jim thought he could handle himself in the woods, but he had never seen a man whose moccasined feet could move so swiftly, with so little noise.

The boy lay there listening with all his might, but for several minutes the only sound he heard was the light rustle of the breeze above in the beech leaves. At last he caught the faint, querulous call of the turkey-hen somewhere beyond the low hill to the right, and after an interval of a few seconds, the banging report of a gun. Again he waited, half expecting a second shot, for he knew that wild turkeys were elusive things to kill. But instead the next sound that reached him was a cheerful whistle that grew louder as the hunter approached. Dodo raced away barking and a moment later returned, more excited than ever.

Jim saw why, when Jacques appeared, for he was carrying over his shoulder the body of a huge bronze-feathered turkey-cock.

The boy half raised himself on his bed. "Golly," he murmured in admiration, "that's the biggest gobbler I ever saw! But it was a hen turkey that was calling, wasn't it?"

The woodsman laughed. "The first time, yes," he said. "The second time I myself called, and this fellow came walking up to my gun."

"Aren't you going to make a picture of him?" the boy asked.

Jacques shook his head. He had already set about plucking and dressing the bird. "I have drawn wild turkeys many times," he answered. "Some day I will show you, when you come home with me to Mr. Pirrie's plantation."

Jim lay quiet awhile, wondering at this strange man. He seemed a polished gentleman in spite of his rough clothes and his evident familiarity with the wilderness. At length the boy could control his curiosity no longer. "Which are you," he asked, "an artist or a hunter?"

Jacques tipped back his head in another of those infectious laughs. "I am a dozen things—all different. And not a grand success at any of them—yet." He spitted the turkey on the iron rod and built a hot blaze under it. When the fire was going well he turned to Jim once more.

"As you see," said he, "I am by no means an old man. Yet I have been a city merchant, a backwoods storekeeper, a portrait painter, a teacher of the violin—of the dance—of drawing—even of the French language. I am also a parent and a husband, miserably unworthy. But the thing I want to be most of all, perhaps"—and his face grew serious—"is a naturalist. Wherever I go, whatever else I do, I study birds and draw them."

He paused a moment, looking at the fire. Then his face brightened. "Now you know all about me," he said. "But of you I know only that you are not what you appear to be—a desperado. Do you feel strong enough to talk, now? I should like to hear your story."

Jim's body was still weak, but he found speech was no longer an effort. So he lay back on his blanket and told of the adventures that had befallen him since that morning of his birthday. It was hard to realize that so many things had happened in less than four months.

The hunter-naturalist nodded understandingly as the tale progressed. When Jim had finished he gave the turkey a turn on the spit and looked back at the boy with a smile.

"And now what do you want to do—when you are well and strong again?" he asked.

"The thing I want most, right now," said Jim, considering, "is to get home to Rhode Island."

"And grind wheat in the mill?" asked Jacques.

Jim shook his head. "Not for very long," he answered. "I'm a sailor, I guess. I'll go to sea again."

"Good!" cried the woodsman. "Stick to it, my friend. I know something of your feeling. My father was an officer in the navy of France. It would have pleased him if I, too, had followed the sea. Now, my boy, I'll give you another drink of this broth, and then you must rest. The turkey is too big to be roasted quickly. But before night I promise you a feast."

Jim snoozed comfortably through most of that afternoon, and when he opened his eyes at dusk, he was almost himself again. The odor of the sizzling brown fowl over the coals woke him up with a ravenous appetite.

"That smells good!" he said. "When can I have some?"

Jacques rose from his drawing-bench and took the

roast off the fire. "It has been done for an hour past, but I would not wake you," he said. "Too well done in some parts, I am afraid. Still, there is plenty of meat, and your little Dodo can have the over-brown bits."

He cut into the turkey with his hunting-knife, and in a moment Jim was enjoying a huge, tender slab of breast meat. When they had eaten their fill, the woodsman cut off the better parts of the bird, removed the bones, and packed the meat in a small canvas sack.

That evening in the glow of the camp-fire, he showed Jim the finished drawing of the Mississippi kite and several others that he had made in the past few days. It seemed that he was taking a holiday from his regular occupation. He had been engaged for the summer to teach painting to the daughter of a wealthy planter, Mr. James Pirrie, of Oakley, near Bayou Sara. And now, as the young lady had gone away on a visit, he was free to follow his bird studies for a couple of weeks.

"This part of Louisiana is the finest country for birds I have seen anywhere in America," Jacques said, enthusiastically. "A dozen new species I have found, never named before by any naturalist. And many others, usually rare, are abundant here throughout the Spring. Look, I will show you!"

He brought out of his case a handful of small sketches and laid them out in the firelight.

"Here is the yellow-throated wood warbler that sings in the canebrakes," he said, pointing to one of the studies. "This one shows a pair of bay-breasted wood warblers. And this little blue fellow is called the cerulean wood warbler because of his color."

He held up one picture with a look of pride. "Bewick's wren," he explained. "One of the rarest. I had trouble aplenty in finding him."

Among the sketches was a large one that showed a beautiful hawk in flight. Its head and crest were a deep bluish gray-black and its back a slaty blue barred with brown, while the throat was pure white, shading into a reddish white spotted with brown on the breast and thighs. The hawk's feet were a bright lemon yellow, and its hooked beak blue-black at the tip and pale green close to the head. The artist had caught a look of speed and ferocity in the bird's pose that moved Jim to ask a question about it.

"Ah, yes!" exclaimed Jacques. "The peregrine falcon —fastest and fiercest of all the hawk tribe, small though he is. You know how swiftly wild ducks fly? He can catch them in the air! When I shot him he was high up in the fork of a dead tree dining on a mallard he had killed that was twice his size. Look at his talons—huge and sharp and strong—built to seize his prey in flight. That is why he is also called the great-footed hawk."

The woodsman put away his drawings and came back to Jim's side. "You look no longer like a pirate," he smiled. "Go to sleep now, and in the morning, if you feel like it, we will hunt."

XVIII

IM stretched his arms to the morning sunlight, then stood up and tried his legs. To his delight, they bore his weight without weakness.

Jacques was down the hill, washing at a little spring, and the boy joined him there.

"Oho," the hunter greeted him. "Walking, eh? Take it gently awhile, my friend, and then we shall see. You feel strong, but too much work today might set you back."

He looked at the cut in Jim's head, which he had anointed with turkey grease the night before, and found it healing nicely.

When Jim had washed, they ate a breakfast of corn bread and coffee and prepared to break camp. Jacques packed his drawing-board and papers with loving care. The rest of the duffel he flung together in the blanket and rolled up. When all was ready and the embers of the fire had been quenched with dirt, the woodsman paused and looked at Jim. "I can show you now," he said, "how to go from here to Bayou Sara. You are well enough to reach it easily in a day. On the other hand—" he hesitated—"I think we get on well together. I would not wish to delay you a moment in reaching your home, but I should be delighted to have your company. And it may be that through Mr. Pirrie I can help you on your way."

There was such straightforward courtesy in the man's speech that Jim would have had a hard time refusing him if he had wanted to. As it was, he felt he would like nothing better than to stay another week with him. He had never been more powerfully drawn to any one than to this stranger who had saved his life.

"I'll be mighty glad to go with you," he grinned. "And maybe I'll come in handy, carrying one of those packs."

So it was agreed, and Jim took the blanket roll and the ax, while Jacques shouldered the case of drawings and the gun.

Jim had no shoes, but his feet had been toughened by the *White Angel's* deck planks, and he had little difficulty in keeping pace with his companion. They bore southward over rolling red-soiled hills that were covered with a tall growth of magnolia and holly and beech and lofty yellow poplar. It was a rich, wild country, but not at all like the rank, semi-tropical jungles that Jim had fought his way through along the coast.

Every now and then Jacques would stop suddenly in

his tracks and lift a warning hand. His hearing was extremely keen, and he could catch a strange bird-note amid the chirping and whistling of innumerable familiar songsters. Whenever he heard something that interested him he quickly slipped out of the strap that held his pack and ran toward the sound. Stooping low, under cover of the brush, he would move without noise till he was close enough to see the bird plainly or take a shot at it. He never killed a bird wantonly or merely to prove his prowess, but if it turned out to be a species he had not yet had a chance to draw, he might spend an hour in studying its movements and habits before bringing it down. When he did burn powder he rarely missed. Jim had never seen a finer gun or surer marksmanship.

It was during one of these sorties that the pair witnessed as strange a happening as one could imagine. The woodsman had been a few yards in the lead when he saw a flicker of bright plumage in a tree top to the left. He motioned to Jim, and leaving their duffel in the trail, they hurried through the undergrowth in the direction the bird had taken. When they thought they must be near its lighting-place, Jacques squatted by the foot of a tree and sat perfectly still, with Jim crouching beside him. They had been there what seemed a long time—possibly five or six minutes—when there came a sudden rustle in the grass close by.

Out of the thicket jumped a gray squirrel. It went bouncing across the little glade in long leaps—not stopping to look about with a squirrel's usual caution, but quite evidently fleeing for its life. For a second Jim did not see what was chasing it. Then Jacques whispered, "Look!" And Jim, staring along his pointing finger, saw a big brownish snake racing through the grass in pursuit. The reptile went like the flick of a whip, half its five feet of length in the air. And fast as the squirrel ran, it could not gain on its enemy.

On the other side of the glade the fleeing animal reached the foot of a tall poplar tree and dashed up it desperately. To Jim's amazement he saw the snake follow right up the trunk. Its progress was slower than that of the four-footed beast, but it moved with a smooth sureness that sent cold shivers down the boy's back. The squirrel cowered in the top branches till its foe was more than halfway up, then scurried out on a twig and across to the limb of another tree. Instantly the snake, too, changed its direction, darting along a lower branch, holding by its tail and swinging sinuously over a gap of a yard or more to catch the opposite limb in its folds.

Once more the squirrel clung in a high crotch, watching the snake's movements with fixed, beady eyes. And once more the snake began its leisurely ascent. At last the little gray beast gave a terrified leap, spreading its legs and wide, furry tail to break its fall, and struck the ground with a jarring thud. The hunting reptile seemed to have been awaiting this very maneuver, for it, too, dropped while the squirrel was in the air, and landed a split second after its prey. That was the end of the chase. Before the squirrel could gather itself to escape, the snake's head flashed out and its jaws gripped the animal by the nape of the neck. So quickly that Jim could hardly follow its movements, it wrapped coil after coil around its struggling victim.

There was a sharp, gasping cry from the squirrel, and for a moment the crushing folds of the serpent were locked and motionless. Then, with maddening deliberation, it loosed the dead animal and set about swallowing it. Starting at the tail, it worked the hind quarters of the beast into its mouth, stretching its jaws wider and wider. Once the rump was in its throat, the snake seemed to have little difficulty in forcing down the rest of the body.

As the reptile lay coiled there in the sun, distended with its meal, Jacques rose quietly and tiptoed toward it. He held a short club in his hand. It was not until he had come within three or four yards that the snake noticed his approach. It lifted its head lazily and its tail gave a warning *whir!* But in a single bound the woodsman reached it and brought his stick down across the ugly snout. By the time Jim arrived the snake was dead.

"But look here!" the boy cried in astonishment as he bent above it. "This is a rattlesnake! I never knew they could climb like that! See—he's got nine, ten—eleven rattles on his tail."

Jacques was busy slitting open the serpent's belly. He nodded as he heard Jim's exclamation. "Yes," he said, "many a naturalist would tell you that rattlesnakes never climb. Yet here is positive proof. I have seen it happen before, in smaller trees and bushes. At Oakley I will show you a drawing I made of a pair of mocking-birds defending their nest from a big rattler."

With another stroke of his hunting-knife he laid the snake open and there they saw the squirrel lying smooth and whole, with even its hair apparently undisturbed. Jim cut off the snake's rattles to keep as a souvenir. And after a vain search for the bird that had led them to this odd spectacle, they went back to the trail.

The direction Jacques was taking led off to the southeast toward the lower land. There were several kinds of birds to be found among the bayous and canebrakes that he still needed for his collection.

As they walked, he told Jim stories of the habits of wild things and of his adventures in hunting and studying them. He was always modest in telling of his own deeds, but the boy soon discovered that his friend had been through plenty of thrilling experiences. He had several times encountered bear and cougar in the swamps, and once he had come extremely near death at the hands of an outlaw family in the backwoods of the Ohio River country. To Jim's intense delight he found that years before, in Kentucky, Jacques had hunted with the great Daniel Boone himself. He recounted some of Boone's own stories of his skirmishes with the Indians in the early blockhouse days. And he told of various feats the old pioneer had performed with his rifle.

"At a hundred paces," said the naturalist, "Colonel Boone could bark a squirrel. You know what that means? It is to strike the bark of the limb on which the squirrel sits and knock him to the ground, stunned, without damaging the hide or drawing blood. I saw him do it, and he was an old man then, though hale and strong as any youth."

One noon they had come out of the woods and were skirting the fields of a big plantation. A score or more of the field hands were at work in the high cotton, bending low and humming in a throaty harmony as they toiled. A bearded white man in a broad-brimmed straw hat sat his horse at the end of a row and occasionally shouted an order to the slaves. "Hyah, you Sam, buckle down to it!" he would yell, or "Milo, yo' wuthless black scamp, git ovah on the nex' row!"

Half a mile away, across the fields, a big white house, flanked by many-pillared verandas, stood graciously among the trees. Jacques saw it and paused, looking at Jim. "I think," said he, "that some other food than turkey might be a fine thing for you, my friend."

In spite of the boy's expostulations he led the way toward the mansion. A gorgeous peacock screamed and strutted on the terrace, and bright flowers glowed in the sun. When they reached the house Jim saw his friend the woodsman in a new light. He seemed to care nothing for their rough-and-ready appearance but went directly to the door and asked pleasantly for the master. In another moment his courtly address won them a cordial reception.

"I am a wandering artist," he explained to the tall, distinguished-looking man who greeted them. "My friend and I stopped as we passed to admire your beautiful peacocks and wondered if we might not rest a moment here in the shade of your magnolias."

They were not only made welcome with true Southern hospitality, but bidden at once to join the family at luncheon. It was a delicious meal, served in the lavish style of the period, and Jim was fully prepared to do it justice. At first he was blushingly conscious of his ragged clothing, but Jacques gave such a droll explanation of his predicament that he soon felt at ease and laughed with the rest.

When the planter heard of Jim's escape from the *White Angel* he gave a whistle of surprise. "Indeed you were fortunate, young man, to make off when you did," he exclaimed. "If I don't mistake, that was the name of the slaver wrecked near the mouth of Pearl River in the recent hurricane. I had news of it from a friend of mine, a dealer in blacks, who came up from the city two days ago. And by the way, if you are going on to the southward, I'd advise you both to keep an eye out for runaway niggers. It seems a few of them broke free when the ship ran aground—wild blacks, straight from the bush. They've been reported in the swamp country over beyond Lake Maurepas."

"Thanks for your warning," smiled Jacques. "We are going in that direction, yes. But we shall hardly get within thirty or forty miles of the place you mention. I hope to find my birds in the Amite River bottomlands. At any rate we shall keep a careful lookout in case the poor devils cross our trail. No doubt they're starving by this time."

As the party rose from the table the planter called Jim aside. "You are going into swampy country, my lad," he said, "country where moccasins and other poisonous snakes abound. I have an old pair of riding-boots that should fit you. Suppose we look them over." He led the way into a small room hung with rods, guns, and hunting trophies, and produced the boots from the closet. Jim found them almost exactly the right size when he pulled them on. He tried to put his gratitude into words, but the Southerner waved him aside with a smile. "They'll hold together till you get back to Pirrie's plantation," he said.

In the drawing-room they found the ladies in a delighted semicircle around Jacques, who was playing a lively French air on a violin. And a moment later the accomplished woodsman laid the fiddle aside and spread out before them his sketches of birds.

The afternoon was well along before the two wanderers could take their departure. "I owed them something in return for our entertainment," Jacques explained. "It is the only payment I can make."

They made camp that night on a knoll, five or six miles to the east of the plantation, and in the morning the naturalist was up as usual at daybreak, listening to the first burst of bird-song. Jim, too, had come to wait eagerly for those dawn choruses that filled the woods. Except for his pigeons at home, he had never paid much attention to birds. But now he was beginning to catch some of the infectious enthusiasm of his companion.

Several times as they journeyed that day, it was he, instead of the sharp-eyed woodsman, who sighted flitting strangers in the trees. And in a dark little crevice in the rocks near their noonday fire, Jim found a dingy reddish-brown bundle of feathers that turned out to be a sleeping whippoorwill—or at least, so the boy named it.

But Jacques shook his head. "Your northern whip-poorwill is never found here in Louisiana," he said. "This bird is bigger and has more red on the head and back. They call him the chuck-will's-widow from his song. Listen." And he whistled the mournful series of notes that Jim remembered hearing in the dusk along the bayous. "That song," Jacques concluded, "he sings only at twilight—never by day."

Later that afternoon they descended a gentle slope and found themselves at the edge of the swamp. The whole country had changed in the last five miles. There were no more hills or open hardwood groves. The rank jungle before them was broken only by still black pools of water. Dodo sniffed uneasily along the brink and came back to Jim, looking up at him with troubled eyes. The boy laughed. "Thinking about those alligators—aren't you, dog?" he asked.

Jacques retraced his steps for a hundred yards or more. "We will camp back here on the higher ground," said he. "I expect I shall find all the birds I want close by, so we may as well stay a day or two."

Jim cut a dozen poles and made a rough lean-to shelter while his companion was building the fireplace and getting their supper started. By the time darkness fell they had a snug little camp, complete even to beds of leaves on which to spread their blanket.

The woodsman stretched his arms with a mighty yawn and lay down at Jim's side. In three minutes his slow, even breathing gave evidence that he was asleep. But somehow the boy was restless that night. He could see Dodo, black against the red embers of the fire, sitting watchful, with one ear cocked toward the southeast. There was no breeze to break the sultry spell of the heat. Jim lay quiet and listened drowsily to the night noises—the intermittent bass chorus of bullfrogs in the swamp, the cheep and flutter of a roosting bird, the movements of small soft-footed animals among the trees. After a time he became aware of another sound, fainter but steadier than all the others. It was so indistinct that it might have been his own heart pounding—a slow, pulsing throb—*boom*—wait—*boom*—wait—*boom*—on and on. Somewhere, far off through the dark, a drum was being beaten.

XIX

OR five minutes or more Jim lay listening to that almost imperceptible sound before he was sure it was not merely his imagination. Then he reached cautiously over and touched his bedfellow.

Jacques was sleeping so soundly that Jim had to nudge him several times and finally call his name before he roused him. "Listen!" whispered the boy when Jacques was awake at last. And for a long moment they sat there without breathing, straining their senses to catch the sound.

"It's stopped," Jim exclaimed. "I'm sure I heard it—a sort of drumming, very faint." They both listened again, but the noise, whatever it might be, was no longer audible.

Jacques laughed. "Perhaps it was the fairies," he suggested, "or a woodpecker at work on a hollow tree. If so it is a new species, nocturnal in its habits, and we should get one. No, my friend, I think your ears have played a trick on you. It may be a small return of your fever."

Jim was doubtful now himself. "Well," he said, "I guess it was nothing to worry about, or Dodo would have growled. I'm sorry I woke you, Jacques."

In the brilliant sunshine of the next morning the incident seemed so absurd that both of them chuckled over it. When breakfast was over, the woodsman set up his drawing-board on a fallen log in the shade of a huge magnolia tree.

"I have several birds here that I must draw," he said. "And in the meantime we need fresh meat. Take the gun, Jim, and see what you can find. A squirrel or two—a turkey—perhaps some ducks—any of them would be a pleasant addition to our larder."

"Right!" answered Jim with alacrity. "I'll be back with a dinner before noon. Have a fire going, and the meat will be here!"

The boy was in high spirits as he set off through the woods. The morning was still cool enough to make walking pleasant, and Jim was delighted at the opportunity to use his comrade's gun. It was a beautifully balanced French fowling-piece with a trigger guard and cheek plate of chased silver. He had cleaned and loaded it with care, and now he carried it ready under his arm as he swung across the sun-flecked glades.

Dodo scurried busily ahead or to either side, sniffing at all the telltale animal scents that crossed his path. The spaniel seemed as eager as his master to prove his prowess as a hunter. "Huh!" Jim jeered. "Might think you were a real trail dog, to look at you!"

Small birds flitted everywhere around them as they went, but the game they sought kept out of sight. Jim had chosen to strike back away from the swamp, both because the traveling was easier and because the openness of the woods offered better chances for unhampered shooting.

They must have traversed nearly three miles when Jim heard a sound of something moving in the thicket a hundred yards ahead. There was a rustle and the snap of a branch and then quiet. Instantly Dodo grew wildly excited. He ignored Jim's whispered command to be silent and dashed ahead, barking his loudest. The boy gave a hurried look to his priming and ran after. Just then he was heartily regretting the impulse that had moved him to bring the dog. But an instant later he changed his mind.

In the middle of the thicket he came on the body of a half-grown fawn. Blood was still flowing from a great gash torn in its throat, and when he touched its warm side he realized it had been killed only the moment before. Hastily Jim looked around him. The animal that had slain the young deer could not be far off, and judging from the wounds it had inflicted, he had no wish to meet it unprepared.

Dodo was still barking furiously, a dozen yards away. The boy held his gun ready and pushed forward through the brush. As he approached the dog he became aware of a low, snarling sound above him and looked up to see a big, gray-furred beast crouching on a tree limb twenty feet from the ground. Yellow eyes blazed angrily from its slim feline head, and as it snarled it showed a formidable array of white teeth. No second glance was needed to tell Jim that this was a cougar—a painter, as it was called in the backwoods. He had heard enough about the strength and ferocity of the huge cats to know that he could never hope to kill one with a charge of bird-shot. On the other hand he knew that the cougar would stay treed as long as Dodo kept up his barking.

Quickly the boy went back to the dead fawn. He drew his hunting-knife and cut the two haunches from the carcass, slipping a green stick through the hamstrings to make them easier to carry. Then he left the thicket as he had entered it, and when he had gone a little distance he whistled for Dodo. After giving vent to a few final warnings, the spaniel came tearing out of the underbrush, immensely pleased with himself.

Jim looked back, as they took up the trail toward camp, and saw the cougar watching them from the edge of the thicket. The big beast returned the boy's stare for a moment, then turned and slipped out of sight in the direction of the dead fawn.

"That was a good job, little dog," Jim told the spaniel. "Plenty of nice fresh meat without wasting a shot!"

With the trained woodsman's instinct he followed his own back-track, picking up, one after another, the landmarks that he had unconsciously noted. Once he left the trail to take a shot at a flock of wild pigeons. The birds flew overhead and settled in a clump of trees to his right. And with two shots he was lucky enough to bring down three of them before they took wing again.

It was approaching noon when Jim came over the last rise and started down the hill toward camp. He was hot and tired but proud of the proceeds of his hunting. A pleasant smell of wood smoke came drifting up to him from the fire.

"Ho, Jacques!" he shouted. "Get ready to eat!"

The words went echoing through the woods, but no answering call came back to him. "Guess he's gone off after water or something," Jim told the dog.

He laid down his gun in front of the shelter and looked about. The fire had burned low. It was while he was in the act of putting more wood on the embers that something strange caught his eye. The artist's drawing-board lay on the ground beside the log and the sketch fastened to it was torn half across and rumpled. Jim stood up and looked around uneasily. For the first time he realized that something had happened here during his absence. The ground showed evidences of a scuffle. Near the entrance of the lean-to he found a torn piece of brown linen trodden into the earth. And though the big portfolio of drawings was apparently untouched, the blanket was gone from their leaf bed.

Jim was thoroughly alarmed now. He was about to raise his voice in another shout when he heard Dodo growling somewhere behind the shelter. Seizing his gun, the boy ran to the spaniel's side and found him nosing at an object half buried among the leaves. It was a piece of heavy wood, shaped into a long, thin oval, and sharpened to a knifelike point at one end. The sides, too, had been scraped to a keen, ugly-looking edge, and at the end opposite the point was a dangling remnant of sinew, taken from the body of an animal.

For a moment Jim balanced the thing in his hand, puzzled by some vaguely familiar feature of its shape. Then suddenly he remembered. He had seen just such an implement, topping the shaft of a weapon carried by a native warrior on the Guinea coast. It was an African spearhead!

Fear clutched at the boy's heart as he remembered the warning given them by the planter two days before. In a flash of understanding he knew that the throbbing drum of last night had been no illusion. The sunlit silence of the woods suddenly became menacing—treacherous.

With hands that shook a little, Jim reloaded the fowling-piece, ramming home an extra charge of powder. "Now, Dodo," he muttered, "we've got to depend on that nose of yours. Where did they go, boy? Find 'em!"

He still held the tattered piece of his friend's hunting-shirt that he had found by the campfire. Now he put it under the spaniel's nose, trying with all his might to convey his meaning to the wise little dog. Dodo wagged his tail eagerly and went bounding off as if he thought it was a game. In a moment he came back with a piece of stick in his mouth.

"No, no." Jim shook his head, exasperated. "I'll have to find the trail myself." And he set out on a slow circuit of the camp, hunting for some clew that might show him which direction Jacques' captors had taken.

He found it sooner than he expected—a freshly broken twig beside a flattened place in the grass that might have been a footprint. It was on the lower side of the lean-to, toward the swamps. The boy waited for no more, but clutched his gun and started. The track, now that he had found it, was not hard to follow. Dodo came running to his master after a moment and put down his nose with a growl that showed he understood at last what they were doing. In places where Jim was baffled by lack of visible signs, the spaniel led the way at a steady trot.

The trail skirted the edges of marshy pools and avoided the thicker masses of jungle. After a mile or more it plunged into a canebrake, and here the boy went swiftly, for the path the party had taken was plainly marked. There must have been four or five of them, he thought, to have bent so much of the cane. But whether they were carrying the woodsman with them he could not tell. He fervently hoped they were, for if Jacques were still alive there might be a chance to save him.

At last, hot and panting, he came out of the tall cane and found himself in a clump of thick-growing trees, festooned with moss, at the edge of a bayou. Here the trail seemed to lead to the left. Jim was not sure at first, but after going a score of yards along the bank he saw another shred of brown linen, caught on a bramble, that heartened him and quickened his stride.

Fast as he went, however, Jim moved with more caution now. He had covered five or six miles in his pursuit, and it was not likely that those he was trailing had had more than an hour's start. If they were aware that he was following, he might walk into an ambush at any moment.

The boy and his dog had followed the twisting shore of the bayou for perhaps half a mile when Dodo, in the lead, stopped suddenly by the edge of the water and threw up his head in a challenging bark. Hastily Jim silenced him and listened, fearful that the noise might have betrayed them. Many seconds elapsed, before any sound broke the stillness, and then it was only the song of a bird somewhere far off across the bayou. Jim was casting about for the trail when the bird's call came again—the low, mournful notes of a chuck-will's-widow. Quietly the boy crouched among the bushes, his heart pounding hard. That song, Jacques had told him only yesterday, was never heard except at twilight. And now

the sun was still high in the sky. It was his friend sig-
naling to him from the woods on the other side of the
bayou. It meant either that he had escaped and was in
hiding or that he was imprisoned somewhere out of sight
of his captors but too near them to risk a shout.

With tremulous lips, Jim attempted to reply to the
whistle. He went over the call very softly at first, then
louder as he caught the right notes. And in a moment the
answer came back to him. Now to cross the bayou. It
was very narrow at this spot—hardly more than fifteen
feet, Jim thought, measuring it with his eyes. But he
knew that Dodo, after his experience with the alligators,
would never be willing to swim it. He took the spaniel
by the skin of his neck and back, swung him twice to
gain momentum, and tossed him with all his strength
toward the other bank. The little dog landed in the edge
of the water and scrambled quickly out. He made no outcry but shook himself and looked back at Jim with re-
proachful eyes. At once the boy waded into the dark,
sluggish stream. Holding the gun and powder-horn above
his head, he swam a few strokes and was across in a jiffy.

The faint bird-call still came at intervals from deep
in the forest beyond. Jim whispered again to the dog to
keep quiet, and tiptoed toward the sound as silently as
he could move.

XX

HE boy had no time to be frightened as he stole forward. His whole attention was centered on reaching Jacques without being himself discovered. It seemed an interminable distance that he had to fight his way through the jungle. There was no trail here. He moved solely by the guiding call of the chuck-will's-widow. At last he knew he was very close. Hardly daring to breathe, he crawled through a dense thicket and came on a tiny open space screened on every side by brush. And there was Jacques. Bare to the waist, the woodsman sat on the ground with his back against a sapling, his wrists bound tightly behind the trunk with strips of his own hunting-shirt.

Softly Jim whistled the bird's call, and his friend's head came up with a jerk. His eyes glowed gratefully, but his lips formed a warning sign of silence. There was no guard in sight. The boy darted across to Jacques' side, laid down the fowling-piece, and pulled out his knife. He was just slashing the last of the bonds that held his comrade's arms when a sudden yelp from Dodo made him whirl about. And there, towering above him, was a gigantic naked black man with a spear in his hand.

Before either Jim or the naturalist could make a move the negro stooped and picked up the gun. Then he stood, huge and impassive, scowling down upon them. His face was fiendishly masked with broad smears of red and white clay, but even before Jim saw the fresh-healed scar in the black's shoulder, he knew him.

After a moment the mighty negro lifted his head and shouted a single word. No voice answered, but soon there were sounds in the bush and three more blacks came bounding into the glade. They jabbered excitedly when they caught sight of Jim, but at another brief command from the chief they were silent. He handed the gun to one of his followers and turned to the white men with an abrupt gesture. "Come," he said, in English, and they rose obediently. A few seconds later the party was on the march again, the giant chief and another negro in the lead, then Jim and Jacques, with Dodo trotting beside them and another pair of bucks bringing up the rear.

So they tramped for a mile or more, along cunningly hidden paths that threaded a narrow way between treacherous morasses. In single file as they were, there was little chance for talk. But once when there was a second's pause Jacques turned and whispered to Jim, "It was very brave and very foolish of you to come, my friend. You should never have done it. Now the torture will be for two of us."

Jim's face was pale, but he said nothing. A little way ahead he could see a low knoll covered with trees. To all appearances it was an island surrounded by impassable swamps. But the blacks moved toward it, zigzagging from one hummock to the next as surely as if they followed a highroad. Dodo began barking violently, and the nearest savage turned on him with lifted spear. Jim caught the dog by the scruff of the neck and stopped his noise, or he might have been stabbed to death at once.

They went up the side of the knoll amid a silence that was unnatural. No birds sang. And this sinister quiet made all the more startling the sound that came to them as they reached the top of the hill. It was the sudden lusty cry of a baby, stifled almost before it had begun. They bent low to pass through a sort of tunnel cut through a thick mass of vines and creepers. And beyond it they emerged in a neatly cleared space fifty feet or more in diameter. At the farther side were two small cane-thatched huts that looked as if they had been transplanted from the middle of Africa.

The chief strode out to the middle of the open space and clapped his hands. A scantily clad old negress came from one of the huts and stared at the white captives with rolling eyes. The big black spoke to her in a gruff monosyllable, and she went scurrying to fetch wood from a heap at the side of the clearing.

While the old crone was building a fire, the bucks brought a length of tough, limber grapevine and tied Jim and Jacques together, back to back. Their knives had already been taken from them. Jim tested the strength of their bonds cautiously, but the knotted vine held firm, and one of the black warriors, seeing the tensing of the boy's muscles, grinned at him malignantly.

The giant leader of the escaped slaves was busy in the meantime. He had Jacques' knife in his hand and was methodically sharpening the end of a long hardwood stake. There was something so horrible in these preparations that Jim felt cold and sick. But he set his teeth hard and kept from trembling. Behind him he felt his comrade's hand touch his own with a firm, reassuring grip. A barely perceptible murmur reached his ears. "At the end," Jacques was whispering, "we will bend our backs—break loose—die fighting, not by fire."

The old woman had laid the wood in a high conical pile near the center of the cleared area. Now she went to the hut and brought out a rough clay pot filled with smoldering coals.

The chief sheathed the knife and stood balancing the heavy stake judicially in his hand. He gave another of his gruff orders then, and two of his men sprang forward, seizing each of the prisoners by the arm. Jim's head buzzed. He felt himself sway dizzily on legs that had suddenly gone slack. But he did not fall, for at that instant there was a piercing scream from the door of the second hut. He struggled back to consciousness and opened his eyes to see a young negro woman standing there with a child at her breast. She was speaking—pointing at him—shaking her head.

The chief crossed to her in three long strides. For a moment he appeared angry, as if he wished her to go back. Then something she was saying caught his attention. He let his hand fall and turned, staring at Jim with amazement written on his face. He asked the woman a question and she answered, nodding vigorously.

The giant negro came forward slowly, his eyes still fixed on the white boy. He drew the knife once more and cut the vine rope that bound the captives. Then he knelt on the ground and placed one of Jim's hands on his bowed head.

Jacques had been facing the other way with his back toward the huts. Now he swung about, and his mouth fell open in blank astonishment at the scene he witnessed. Jim's own wits had been scattered by the suddenness of this turn in their fortunes. But at least he understood the reason for it. For he had recognized the young negress as the woman to whose baby he had given water, that last afternoon aboard the slave-ship.

The boy took his hand from the big black's head and caught him by the arm, lifting him up. For a moment the chief strove to speak, but the word or two of Engglish he knew was wholly inadequate to the situation.

With a beckoning motion of his arm he called his wife to his side. Her face was wreathed in smiles.

"He say you go now," she gesticulated. "No kill 'em white man. You save 'em baby. All same now save 'em one-two white feller."

Jacques gasped. "*Mon Dieu!*" he muttered, lapsing into his native tongue. "It is wonderful!" One of the blacks had already handed him his gun and the blanket. But when the chief attempted to return the hunting-knife as well, the woodsman made a graceful gesture of refusal. "Keep it, my friend," he said. "You must have need of such tools here."

Jim and his comrade were free now, but they were not allowed to depart at once. With a great deal of bustling to and fro the old woman lighted a fire—a much smaller one than the pyre she had first built—and started preparing a meal. When it was ready the men, white and black, sat down with some solemnity around a big central gourd of food, and politely dipped their hands in the stew, after the chief. It was made, Jim thought, of rabbit meat and some kind of small fowl, cooked up with herbs and roots. And though they had little appetite just then, the two released prisoners were able to swallow enough to satisfy the etiquette of the occasion.

The afternoon was nearly gone when the boy and his comrade took their leave. One of the negroes went with them as far as the bayou to guide them through the most difficult part of the swamp. After that they trusted to the failing light and Dodo's sense of direction to take them back to camp. It was pitch dark and a slow drizzle of rain had begun to fall when they finally felt their way up to the lean-to.

Both of them were too tired to do much talking that night. They crawled under the shelter, pulled the blanket over them, and went to sleep.

Next morning the weather was still wet, but Jim managed to find enough dry wood to have a fire going before Jacques awoke. The naturalist was stiff from the bruises he had suffered in his struggle with the negroes. And Jim could hardly keep from laughing at the comical picture he made as he limped forth from the lean-to, clutching the blanket around him to hide his nakedness.

"It was the only shirt I brought with me," said Jacques, ruefully. "If it had been given to that poor woman to wrap herself in, that would not be so bad. But to have it torn into ribbons to tie me with—*pouf!*

"Nevertheless, shirt or no shirt, we are extremely well out of that affair. And," he concluded, "to you, Jim, I owe my life. I shall not forget it."

"Huh!" snorted the boy. "Talk about owing lives! Where would I have been now if—"

"It is not the same," Jacques interrupted. "But we will say no more about it now. What is there for breakfast?"

Proudly Jim produced his deermeat and pigeons which, by good fortune, he had hung on a limb before he discovered his friend's disappearance. While the cutlets of venison were broiling, he told Jacques of his meeting with the cougar, and as they ate, the older man gave him an account of his own adventure. Following Jim's departure, he had brought out the drawing-board and gone to work. He had been so deeply engrossed with his sketching that he kept no account of the time, but he thought a couple of hours must have passed before the attack came. The negroes had stolen on him so quietly that he was wholly unprepared.

"Suddenly," said he, "they leaped upon me from behind—two of them. As we wrestled on the ground I broke loose and was getting to my feet when a third ran at me with his spear. Luckily I caught the shaft in my hand and broke off the head. But then came that vast fellow—the chief—and my battle was ended. They trussed me with pieces of my shirt, took the blanket, and set off. You know the rest of the story."

When the meal was over, Jacques looked dubiously at the sky and sniffed the wind. "It acts like a two-day storm," he said. "There'll be few birds about, and I cannot draw in the rain. Let us take the trail, then, back to Oakley."

Jim was doubtful of his friend's fitness to travel, but Jacques scoffed at such an idea. "It will do me good," he laughed, "limber my sore muscles. And in three days, with good fortune, I shall have a shirt to wear!"

So they packed up their belongings once more and set

"SUDDENLY," SAID HE, "THEY LEAPED UPON
ME FROM BEHIND—TWO OF THEM"

out, the woodsman blanketed like an Indian squaw. All day the drizzle continued, but they slept that night under a bushy evergreen tree and pushed on again in the morning. The second day found them in more settled country. Cotton and sugar plantations were all around them, and when evening came they were made welcome at the cabin of a white farmer, with hog and hominy as a change from their diet of wild meat. True to Jacques' promise, the following afternoon the travelers passed the site of the camp where Jim had lain convalescing. "It is only a few miles more," cried the naturalist. *"Courage, mon brave!"*

The sun broke through the western clouds as they neared the Pirrie plantation. An old darky, riding a mule home from the field, caught sight of them—took one look at the two scarecrow figures—and flogged his beast into a wild gallop. He disappeared up the hill in the direction of the quarters, and in a few moments they saw another mounted figure riding down the road. This time the steed was no mule, but as dainty a black saddle-mare as Jim had ever seen. And the rider was a girl with corn-colored hair who swayed with an easy grace in her saddle, flicking her boot with a crop as she cantered to meet them.

At a little distance from the pair she suddenly reined in the mare and burst into a gale of laughter. "Oh, Mr. Audubon!" she cried between spasms. "To think it's only you! Old Juba was scared white. He told us there were a couple of 'ha'nts' coming. But wherever have you been? And why such an outlandish dress?"

Jacques made her a bow. "The blanket," he said, "is for purposes of modesty. I will tell you the whole story later. But first of all, Miss Pirrie, may I introduce my friend Jim Slater, late of New England and the sea."

Jim bowed in turn, dazzled by the young lady's smile.

"Welcome to Oakley, Mr. Slater," said she. "And what a darling dog you've got. But we must hurry if you're both to change for dinner. We have another guest, Mr. Audubon—an old friend of Mother's—a Creole lady from New Orleans who has been visiting in Baton Rouge. I'll go ahead and have the boy lay out some clothes for you."

And with that she spun the mare around and was off toward the house at a gallop.

XXI

IM stood in front of the long glass and wondered if it could be himself he saw imaged there. An hour earlier he had entered this room as tattered and un-couth as a wild man in a circus. Since then he had bathed and put on a complete change of clean raiment sent in by the master of Oakley. And here he was, clad in a fine suit of gray broadcloth, with snowy linen showing above the rich blue cravat at his throat, and the tips of polished shoes shining below his long and elegant pantaloons. His tanned face glowed with all the cleanliness that soap and water could produce, and his hair, bleached by the sun, was smoothly brushed back from his forehead.

There was a knock at his door, and Jacques, also resplendent in fresh clothing, appeared. His eyes widened with delight. "Aha," he said, "our pirate has become very respectable indeed! Shall we go down?"

In the drawing-room Jim was given a stately welcome by James Pirrie and his wife and was introduced to another lady—a wistful-eyed, middle-aged Frenchwoman, clad in black, whose name he did not catch. As they were starting in to dinner, he saw a flash of blond hair on the stairs, and the girl he had seen on horseback tossed him a roguish smile.

"No, Mother, Mr. Slater must sit by me," she insisted when they reached the table. "I'm sure his adventures have been fascinating, and I intend to hear about them from his own lips."

It was a gay meal, for Jacques—or Mr. Audubon, as every one called him—was at his sparkling best. He kept them in gales of merriment with his account of their experiences.

"But, Mr. Audubon," cried the irrepressible Miss Pirrie, when he paused for a moment, "you have not told us how you lost your shirt!"

"That," said Jacques, "must remain one of those unplumbed mysteries," and he smiled across the table at Jim. They had made a compact between them that as far as they were concerned, the escaped negroes should enjoy their freedom in the swamps undisturbed.

In an interval of the more general table-talk, the boy heard a fragment of conversation between the Creole lady and her hostess. She was speaking in quaintly broken English and her voice was low and sad. "No," she said, "there were no survivors. Whether the ship was lost in a storm or taken by the pirates, there is no telling. We do not even know where his body lies—my poor Dieudonné."

The name woke a sudden response in Jim's brain. "Tell me," he said quietly to the girl at his side, "who is she?"

"Madame LeGros," whispered Miss Pirrie, "wife of the Creole shipowner. Her only son was lost at sea."

Jim nodded and was silent. He must have seemed a dull table-companion, for from then to the end of the meal he was absorbed in his own thoughts.

When they returned to the drawing-room for coffee he waited until the Frenchwoman was disengaged and went directly to her side.

"Madame," he said simply, "I heard you mention your son."

"Yes?" she answered, startled. He could see a vague hope in her widening eyes, and hastened to go on.

"It is a sad message that I have for you," he said. "I was with your boy when—he died."

"O-o-h!" she breathed, in a long, whispering sigh.

For a moment Jim fumbled inside his vest and brought out the cameo on its little gold chain. As he looked at the profile so delicately cut in the shell, he realized that it was a likeness of the woman before him.

"He gave me this to bring to you," said the boy, and placed the locket in her hand. Then he squared his shoulders and went through with his task. Briefly and very gently he told the circumstances under which her son had died. "He did not suffer at the last," Jim said. "I gave him water. And he told me to take his gun and his little dog. Probably I owe my life to them—and him. Afterward I dug a grave in the sand and put a cross there."

The lady's hands, folded over the cameo, did not shake, and her voice was steady. "Could you—find the place?"

"Yes," said Jim eagerly. "It must be within twenty leagues of New Orleans."

At that moment there was an exclamation of delight from Miss Pirrie, and the boy turned to see Dodo trotting into the room. The spaniel came toward him, his tail wagging happily. He was reaching up to lick his master's hand when Madame LeGros leaned forward and uttered a sobbing cry—"Dodo!" And with a whine of frantic joy the little dog sprang into her arms.

There was a moment of quiet while the company stood amazed. Then the Creole lady recovered her composure. She smiled at them bravely through her tears. "You must excuse this little scene," she said. "It was seeing my son's dog again that—but never mind." She rose and laid her hand on Jim's arm. "Tomorrow I must go back to the city," she concluded. "We have something to do—this young man and I."

Next morning by nine Jim had packed his few belongings in a little bag and was ready to start on his journey. He insisted on taking Mr. Pirrie's address, so that he might repay him for his clothes when he should have any money. The planter laughed at him but finally agreed.

Jacques was genuinely distressed at seeing his comrade go, though glad of his good fortune. "Alas!" he cried, "I have had no chance to show you all my drawings—the mocking-birds—the wild turkey. But we shall meet again some day when I come to your New England. And as for the drawings, it is my life's hope to see them made into a book. 'The Birds of America'—is it not a grand title? When that book is published, my friend, you shall surely have one, as a remembrance of John James Audubon and of our adventures in the woods."

The carriage came to the door. Farewells were said. And as the coachman gathered his reins the madcap daughter of the house leaned over the wheel and gave Jim a kiss. "So that you won't forget Louisiana!" she called after the furiously blushing youth.

For a day and a night the boy and his new-found patroness voyaged down river in the palatial grandeur of the steamboat's upper deck—that region of elegance that had seemed so unattainable to the wounded stowaway less than a fortnight before. Madame LeGros was no sentimentalist. She rarely spoke of her son to Jim, and when she did she was always calm and matter-of-fact. But she treated the young Rhode Islander with a motherly kindness that touched his heart. He was more eager to see his own mother than he would admit even to himself.

In New Orleans they went at once to the busy offices of Gaston LeGros. He was a rotund little Frenchman with a bald head and keen black eyes. When his wife had told him something about Jim he asked the lad three or four questions, watching him intently as he answered. Then he nodded and rose, gripping him by the hand. "You will bring him back—our poor Dieudonné," he said. "Tomorrow we will fit out a vessel to go at once. And afterward I wish you to talk to me. I have use for just such a young man as you."

So it was that five days later Jim sat once more in the office of the little Frenchman and discussed his future plans. He had guided the captain of a fast-sailing sloop to the hidden cove where he had buried the young Creole by the light of the pirate fire. There they had found the body undisturbed and brought it back with them for decent interment in the LeGros family vault.

The shipowner's voice was husky with emotion as he thanked Jim for this service, and he had to blink his eyes very fast to hide the tears. "But now, my friend," he said at length, "let us talk about yourself. You are ambitious, my wife tells me, to follow the sea?"

Jim replied emphatically that he was. "But," he added, "first of all I ought to tell you that I ran away from home last Spring—and—well, I'd like to go back for a little visit. Maybe you can see how it is, sir—"

"Indeed, yes!" cried M. LeGros. "By all means. I have several ships, trading to different parts of the world, and one of them, the *Belle Etoile*, is sailing next week for Havre, by way of Boston. It happens that there is room in her cabin for a passenger, and I should be delighted—"

"Thank you, sir," Jim smiled, interrupting him, "but if you don't mind, I'd rather ship before the mast. I'm still but a sorry sailor, and if I'm to be a ship's officer one day, I need all the experience I can get."

"You are right, my lad," nodded the Creole. "That was spoken with true Yankee spirit. It is agreed, then. The ship lies over ten days or more in Boston, to discharge cotton and take fresh cargo. That will give you time for your visit. I will arrange it at once with Captain Bonhomme. But in the meantime, my boy, you must stay with us until you sail."

.   .   .

It was the middle of a sleepy August afternoon when Jim Slater drove up the familiar elm-shaded road on the seat of Ben Derry's cart. In his trim blue blouse and glazed hat he was as smart a young tar as one could see in a long day's journey. He had ridden down the post road in state the day before, on top of the Boston-to-Providence coach. He had strolled a trifle superciliously through the small, quaint streets of the town that morning. And now he was going home.

"Ay, lad," the peg-legged carrier was saying, "the old man took on somethin' terrible when he found ye was gone. But he's quieted down a lot. I figger mebbe he'll be sort o' glad to sight your tops'ls, arter all. Well, here we are. I'll be lookin' to ride ye back next week."

There it was—the solid stone house with the ivy climbing up its wall—the drowsily droning mill—the cooing pigeons picking up grain by the horse-rail. With a pounding heart, Jim ran across the yard and flung open the kitchen door. At the sound of his war-whoop, old Martha dropped her paring-knife, her Indian stolidity shattered for once. Her brown face crinkled in an amazed grin as he gave her a bearlike hug.

Then his mother's voice, a little tremulous, came from the next room. "Who's there?" she asked, and the next moment he gave her her answer.

"Your letter came, Jim," she said, when that first long embrace was ended. "It got here two weeks ago, but I only had a chance to read it once. Your father's been carrying it ever since. He's—well—he's not angry any more." She smiled at him and dabbed the tears away with her handkerchief. "Now go find him, while I see what's going to be for supper. My goodness, you must be starved!"

Jim laughed happily. "No, Mother," he answered, "I really have eaten since I went away, even if sometimes it wasn't as regularly as I'd like."

He went out to the mill, entered the open door, and

moved forward through a haze of golden dust to where
a broad, stocky figure stood by the grinding stones. His
father did not hear him till he was by his side. Then he
turned, a slow look of wonder widening his eyes. "Jim!"
he gasped, and in an instant he had gripped the lad in
both his strong arms.

When he had released him, the miller stood back a
pace and looked his son slowly up and down. "A real
sailor!" he said, huskily. "Well, it was in your mother's
blood. I reckon you were bound to be one. And, by gin-
ger"—a thrill of pride crept into his voice—"I'll bet
you'll make a good one!"